The Crossing

a novella by
Rand Eastwood

The Crossing

Cover Art & Interior Design
by Rand Eastwood

Author Website: www.randeastwood.com

ISBN-10: 1-7326546-1-1
ISBN-13: 978-1-7326546-1-7

A Quality Publication by

"Some day you will be old enough
to start reading fairy tales again."

~ C. S. Lewis

The Crossing

What had been a clear blue sky during the heat of the day was now solidly overcast, clouds heaving and churning like boiling pewter as thunderstorms moved in from the south.

Below the turmoil, Tommy Baker stood motionless on the edge of a rocky canyon cliff high above Hope Creek, his black silhouette cut from the steely glare of the molten sky. Alternating tufts of golden and sun-bleached blonde hair gesticulated atop the young boy's head, grappling with the spectral gusts that swirled about him.

The cooler air, pushing ahead of the approaching storm, rustled its way into the tired tree branches, knotted brush, and waist-high grass of the untamed field that lay behind him, and Hope Creek Canyon yawned up at him from below, deep and cavernous, the stench of death on its breath.

Trying to ignore the raspy, speculative whispering of the audience of weeds and dry grass that anxiously observed him from behind, he contemplated the scene that now played out before him.

The dreaded rope bridge.

Old Rope, the locals called it.

And every kid in town feared it.

But I'm not a kid anymore; I'll be thirteen tomorrow.

Thirteen.

A *teenager*.

And *teenagers* aren't afraid of stupid rope bridges...*are they?*

He watched as the bridge shuddered, creaked, and groaned in the rising wind, mocking him as he stood there, petrified.

And he knew that the longer he waited, the worse it was going to get.

As if on cue, in that single moment of hesitation the gusts picked up even more, the storm about to unleash its full fury.

Now Old Rope danced in the wind before him, bidding him—no, *daring* him—to come cross. To Tommy, the perpetual creaking and cracking of all the brittle, decaying ropes that snaked throughout the ancient rickety boards sounded as if they were about to *snap!,* thereby plunging any hapless occupants screaming to their deaths into the rocky canyon below.

Suspicious, the boy sensed trickery: Old Rope was simply waiting, that's all; waiting for him to venture nervously on board, and—once he had traveled too far across, and was just beyond the point of no return—the evil old bridge would gladly let go, laughing as it happily sent Tommy on an unsolicited ride down, all the way to the bottom of the canyon, where the rushing creek skirted around a gauntlet of deadly obstacles: sharp boulders that jutted up from the water like giant stone teeth; partially submerged logs that lay in wait like so many crocodiles; crowded colonies of dead, broken saplings rising into the air like razor-sharp tribal spear traps.

He also knew that if he did go down, and wasn't fortunate enough to be killed instantly on the rocks below—then there were always the turtles and water snakes and carp to finish him off, lurking in hidden cesspools and coves all along the banks of the creek, evil creatures hungrily awaiting just such an opportune feast.

If, that is, he was actually *stupid* enough (or *crazy* enough!) to brave the veritable death trap that dangled haphazardly so high above Hope Creek in the first place.

And in the *wind*, no less...

As the boy contemplated all this, he could barely make out the ominous sound of the rushing creek far below.

Though he was surrounded by the normal sounds of the wilderness—the incessant hiss of cicadas, the birdsong drifting from the woods, the dry grass and weeds sizzling in the wind behind him—he could hear, just beyond all that, something much more sinister: Hope Creek whispering up the canyon walls, the canyon walls relaying the message to Old Rope, and Old Rope beckoning to Tommy...

It was a conspiracy of murderers.

The boy was kicking himself for being so careless earlier in the day, when the stifling summer heat had coaxed old Rope into a still and dormant slumber, and it had been so much easier to cross.

Now he was stuck on the other side, needed to get back across, and was fast running out of time—for nightfall was lurking in the shadows, storm clouds were waltzing in atop the trees, Old Rope was rehearsing its dance of death before him, and the wind was escalating in its intensity with each passing minute.

And he didn't like what he saw.

Not one bit.

•

"Are you ready, Commander Thomas?" Winnie asked, peering intently at his friend through his thick, black plastic-rimmed glasses.

"'That's an affirmative, Commander Winston."

Tommy and his best friend Winnie Milhouse were preparing for what had become a month-long mission: arming themselves with their newly-acquired Wrist-Wrocket slingshots, then venturing out into the uncivilized wilderness (otherwise known as the field on the other side of Hope Creek Canyon) to *shoot stuff*.

For the past month, they'd performed this ritual almost daily—ever since they'd acquired the new weapons in town at Hank's Hobbies & Sporting Gear...

It was the summer of '75, and had been the hottest anyone in the town of Hope could remember. Even the old codgers—who'd been around here for what seemed like *forever,* like before the town was really even a town—lamented this fact as they rocked in their old rockers out on their old wooden porches, puffing on their cigarettes or cigars or corncob pipes:

Yes-sir-ree...this here's the hottest summer I ever seen round these parts...

One day, earlier that summer—end of June, first of July, right in there—the temperature had already hit a hundred degrees by noon, and was threatening to keep right on going, like it was pissed off about something and was cranking it up just to get even.

Tommy was over at Winnie's house. They'd gotten bored playing war with their army soldiers and rubber bands, and Winnie's mom had gone to work for the evening (she worked part-time as a cashier at the old *Gas-n-Grub* gas station and convenience store that occupied the busiest corner of *Railroad Pass,* the small retail center located at the big flashing light where the railroad tracks crossed Main Street up on the north side of town; his dad was a truck driver, so was seldom home, and all Winnie knew was that for the past month, he'd been out on the east coast somewhere), so they decided to ride their bikes into town and see if they could score some fireworks for the Fourth—*real* fireworks, not the lame snakes and sparklers and smoke bombs that most the kids their age had to settle for.

The Milhouses lived in a square white clapboard house, one of an entire row of identical square white clapboard houses that ran along Hillsboro Lane (which Tommy always teasingly referred to as "Hillbilly Lane" in honor of his best friend). Hillsboro Lane was just another crumbling, weed-flanked street in the seedy area of town known as The Flats, a cluster of low-income neighborhoods that were marginalized to the easternmost edge of town, sectioned off by the industrial railroad tracks that ran along its western boundary.

Or, as Tommy would say with a shrug and a smile: "You know—where the hillbillies live!"

From Hillsboro Lane, the boys rode up to the north end of The Flats and turned left onto Homestretch Avenue, a big four-laner that ran east-west all the way through the town of Hope, traversing Town Square downtown and crossing Main Street smack-dab in the middle of Grande Festival Plaza, where all the best shops were (and where it might be busy enough that they could snatch some Black Cats or M-80s or bottle rockets or Roman candles in all the hustle and bustle without getting caught).

The brand-new, jet-black asphalt of Homestretch—they'd just resurfaced it, bright new yellow and white lines and everything—intensified the already stifling heat of the day; it was like riding their bikes around in a black skillet with the stove cranked. Feeling like they were melting in the heat by the time they got to Town Square, they decided to cut south onto Fifth Street before they reached the plaza and stop at Hank's, see about picking up a couple of canteens, then filling them at the water fountain out front of the public library, just down Fifth Street and right on Chapel Lane, across from Hope in Christ church (over the years they had found that for some reason, at that water fountain the water always came out cold, even in the summer, no matter how hot it got).

When they finally reached Hank's, they parked their bikes out front under the awning and hurried inside, both so soaked with sweat they looked like they'd just come in out of the rain.

Heading across the store for the camping and fishing section in the back, they got sidetracked when they spied the shiny new slingshots in the display case up by the register where they kept the pellet and BB guns (which, unfortunately, were out of the question for them; county ordinance said you had to be sixteen to buy those—fifteen if you took and passed the county's gun safety course and were also fortunate enough to get your parents to sign a waiver, yeah right).

Stopping just short of the first aisle—the model train stuff—they discussed it briefly, and were pretty sure the county's age restriction was just for pellet and BB guns, and not for slingshots. With that decided, they about-faced and beelined up to the glass case by the register.

There were three Wrist-Wrockets on display: a metallic red one, a metallic blue one, and an all-silver one—which gleamed so brightly under the fluorescent lights that it looked white. This deception gave the entire showcase a convincingly patriotic look—quite appropriate for the upcoming Fourth of July holiday.

Huddling together, the boys nearly drooled as they peered though the glass, admiring the finely crafted weaponry.

"You boys just gonna stand there foggin up the glass, or you gonna buy somethin?"

Startled, the boys simultaneously jerked their eyes up toward the voice. Hank himself was standing behind the counter, down at the end by the phone. He leaned casually against the wall, big arms across his broad chest, smirking. The office door stood open behind him, revealing an old wooden desk buried under an astonishing array of clutter. Somewhere behind that mess, a smoldering cigarette poured a thin gray stream into the air. Glaring white sunlight from a small window in the back wall cut a white square tube diagonally through the light-blue haze that permeated the entire room.

They were surprised to see him here; finding Hank working the store this early in the day during the summer was unusual. He fished a lot (and, it was rumored, drank a lot) and so his son, Joey—or one of Joey's thug friends from his high school shop class—was usually working, chomping gum at the counter or yakking for hours on the phone or sneaking around the corner for a smoke when business was slow and nobody was looking.

But oddly, Hank was here today.

Probably too hot to fish.

Maybe even too hot to drink.

"They're new," he said as he pushed off the wall with his shoulder and walked over. He was a stocky man, but moved with a smooth, confident gait. Though still solid and muscular, the years had brought on a slight beer gut and slightly receded hair line. His remaining hair, mostly gray now, was pulled back into a ponytail, a defiant stand against his own creeping age, which was proving futile; for even with the ponytail, and even with the platinum ear studs he sported in both ears, his accumulating years were starting to show—the inevitable bags and wrinkles moving in uninvited, there goes the neighborhood.

All except his eyes, that is; his bright, piercing blue eyes seemed ageless; youthful, alert. The one part of him that accurately reflected his perpetually youthful state of mind:

Fifty going on twenty-five.

An avid outdoorsman, his darkly tanned, leathery complexion was amplified by a contrasting short-trimmed silver goatee. Numerous tattoos colored his forearms, some of them military.

He was hands-down the coolest adult Tommy and Winnie had ever met.

As he approached, smiling as always, the two reveled in the ashen smell of cigarette smoke and the manly aroma of cheap cologne that always accompanied him to the counter.

Just as he reached the boys, he stooped and disappeared behind the counter. Then, in a muffled voice:

"You're in luck...just got 'em in yesterday, on the truck."

The boys stared into the glass case, watching in anticipation. The sound of keys jingling, followed by a *click!*, then the mirrored wall in the back of the case suddenly slid open, almost making the boys dizzy as the optical illusion of depth vanished and the back half of the merchandise before them appeared to break away and angle sideways.

Hank retrieved the silver one, stood, and made a show of properly orienting it and placing it carefully on the glass counter in front of them, handling it gently like some rare, delicate artifact.

The boys stared at it, googly-eyed, Winnie's eyes appearing even bigger behind the thick lenses.

Hank pointed an open hand at each feature, the tips of his fingers following along its smooth contours as he spoke:

"Aircraft-grade aluminum alloy frame...maximum-velocity surgical-grade rubber tubing...genuine cowhide pouch—"

—he paused to looked up at the boys, adding: "Comes with an extra one—and an extra set of rubbers, too," then looked back down and proceeded as the boys giggled at the word—

"—precision-molded handle inlayed with high-impact, all-weather neoprene pistol grips..."

Amazed, the boys looked at each other, then turned back.

Hank held it out to Tommy. "Feel how light it is."

Tommy accepted the weapon carefully, with respect.

"Reach up through the wrist support and hold the grip like a pistol. The wrist support rests up here on your forearm, pad on top, with the uprights angled back toward you."

As Winnie watched with envy, Tommy slid his left arm through the wrist support, gripped the handle firmly, then held the weapon out at arm's length. With his right hand, he gently pulled the pouch back, extending the rubber tubing nearly to his shoulder. He closed one eye, sighted down his arm, and pointed the slingshot toward the open office door. He was amazed at how the forearm support enabled maximum extension of the rubber tubes, without putting too much stress on his wrist. Pivoting upward, he moved his aim from the office door to the corner of the ceiling above the entrance.

As Tommy's arm rose, Winnie noticed something near the bottom of the Wrist-Wrocket's handle, and stooped, hands on knees, to get a better look, squinting up at it through his glasses.

Still stooping, he turned to Hank.

"What's the button at the bottom of the handle for?"

Upon hearing this, Tommy relaxed the stretched rubber tubes and flipped the whole thing over, peering at the bottom of the handle.

"Ahhh, very observant, young man," Hank commended, relieving Tommy of the now upside-down weapon. "Watch this."

The boys watched intently as Hank flipped it back to its upright position. They hadn't noticed it before, but they could now see the small domed top of an aluminum button protruding from the backside of the handle just below the grip, centered between the two tubes of the wrist support that extended back toward the user. When he pushed it, a tiny, nearly inaudible *click!* was heard, and Hank folded the wrist support upward against the handle, then pulled the rubber tubes down, hooking the pouch into the crevice that was created by the open hinge.

"Folds for easy storage."

With one hand, he slipped the whole thing casually into his back pocket, then made a show of brushing his hands briskly together, like he had just performed a feat of magic.

"No way!" The boys exclaimed in unison.

"Way," Hank responded quietly, nodding matter-of-factly.

"Now, take a look at this."

As the boys watched, he whisked it out of his pocket, unhooked the pouch, snapped the frame open with a *click!*, then turned it over, placing it upside down on the glass, in much the same way as the boys would do with their bikes whenever they needed to put the chain back on, or fix a flat, or clip some playing cards to the forks along the spokes, or maybe just shine up some old pennies.

With a flick of his wrist, he spun a quarter-sized aluminum cap off the end of the handle, revealing an empty chamber topped with a gleaming, finely machined thread that screamed of quality craftsmanship.

"Ammo storage."

"Whoa," Tommy said as Winnie let out a low whistle.

"And that's not all."

With one hand, Hank flipped the lid into the air like a coin, caught it in his other hand, then held it out to them, displaying a black rubber gasket installed on the inside.

"Waterproof."

"Keeps the rocks dry," Winnie said, nodding.

"Yeah...very cool," Tommy agreed.

"Not rocks."

The boys looked up with puzzled looks just as Hank turned and pulled a small white cardboard box off a shelf behind him. In a series of deft moves, he turned back, slapped the box on the counter, spun it around to face them, and flipped the top back, revealing rows upon rows of shiny steel balls, layered over an inch deep.

"Precision-ground, high-speed stainless steel ball bearings. Handle holds up to forty rounds. There's two hundred to a box, and each unit comes with a box."

The boys looked at each other and smiled, excited.

"So...how much?" Tommy asked.

"Well, lucky for you guys, they're on sale right now for the Fourth, our annual Independence Day Sale. Normally twenty-five, I'm lettin 'em go for twenty. Don't forget, that includes an extra set of rubbers, an extra pouch, and a box of balls—and the balls, bought separately, run four bucks a box, so that's four more dollars you're savin."

Another low whistle from Winnie.

Hank then paused for a moment, leaning with both hands on the counter, tapping one finger on the glass as he looked off into space somewhere, chewing on a thought. Then he looked back to the boys:

"Tell you what—you guys both buy a Wrist-Wrocket, and I'll throw in a coupla boxes of balls, on the house...one extra box for eacha ya."

Hank looked back and forth between the two boys, eyes glowing with youthful enthusiasm—then winked mischievously and clicked his tongue, nodding at them like they were all in on some big secret together.

The boys turned to each other and smiled ear-to-ear.

"That's a good deal," Tommy said pseudo-knowledgeably.

"Yeah—but where we gonna get the money?" Winnie asked.

Screwing the cap back onto the handle, Hank said:

"Well, you boys think it over, then come back and see me when you decide. And don't worry, if the sale's over, I'll go ahead and hook you up with the discount anyway...*if* I have any of 'em left, that is...I expect they'll sell out pretty quick."

With that, he stooped, set the Wrist-Wrocket back into the glass display case, slid the mirrored back door shut, and locked it with a *click!*

The tiny bell tinkled above the boys as they pushed excitedly out of Hank's Hobbies & Sporting Gear and quickly mounted their bikes, hitting the busy street with just one goal in mind: acquiring their new Wrist-Wrocket slingshots as soon as possible!

· It wasn't until they'd pedaled halfway to Grande Festival Plaza in the blazing summer heat that they realized that in their enthusiasm over the Wrist-Wrockets, they'd forgotten all about the canteens.

•

Turns out they weren't able to score any real fireworks that day—and they decided not to waste their money buying any of the stupid kid's stuff either, so they could instead put it toward the eventual purchase of their Wrist-Wrockets.

In the ensuing weeks, the boys did everything they could think of to raise enough money; they pooled their minuscule allowances, swiped abandoned change off of their parent's dressers, and even sold off part of their comic book collections (but not *Captain America* or *Spiderman*—mostly just the lame ones like *Batman* and *The Incredible Hulk*).

They collected discarded bottles and cans all around town, biking heavy, clinking garbage bags-full all the way out to the recycle center on the edge of town next to the dump, where they exchanged them for a few dollars and pocket change.

By August they finally had enough loot to make the neces-sary acquisition, and sped eagerly into town to Hank's. Beating the odds, he was there again (what luck!) and made good on his promise, selling them at the sale price even though the sale had ended after the Fourth. Tommy selected the silver one (no brainer), and Winnie the blue one, and they each got two free boxes of ammo.

They were now set for the rest of the summer—which was getting shorter every day, with school starting back up the very next month.

Back at home, their new Wrist-Wrockets easily made their old homemade slingshots look like toys.

Kid's stuff.

Child's play.

Embarrassed, they bid farewell to their old wooden relics, which had served them so faithfully over the years. They ac-tually held a small military-style funeral, revering the toys as veteran soldiers killed in action as they wrapped them up in newspapers and placed them gently, respectfully, into an old empty shoe box.

Then, pulling down the spring-loaded step ladder, they climbed up into Winnie's attic, and, saluting each other, laid the box to rest inside a large cedar chest, carefully nestling it between piles of old photographs and other memorabilia his family had stored in there over the years.

It was a solemn ceremony, and quite easily justified: arming themselves with mere wood and pebbles simply made them too vulnerable to the enemy.

From here on out, *Commander Thomas* and *Commander Winston* would take to the battlefields armed to the teeth with their new high-tech weaponry, which deployed much faster, more accurate, and highly lethal ammunition.

Real weapons.

Real ammo.

Real soldiers.

•

So today, as always, the boys were operating out of *Command Base One*—otherwise known as Winnie's house, which was the only one even close to their hunting grounds. Tommy lived on a farm out west of town (most days, if he managed to slip away from his dad undetected, Tommy jumped on his bike and headed north on the old County Road 200 that ran past their farm, turned east on Homestretch Avenue, then rode clear across town to Winnie's house. Or, sometimes, he'd walk south about a mile to the train tracks, hop an east-bound freighter across town, and bail on the south end of The Flats, not far from Winnie's house).

So out of necessity, Winnie's house was deemed *Command Base One*. From there the boys could easily walk to the field where they hunted, traveling east through the mostly unfenced yards until they came out on the unmarked, single-lane road that skirts the easternmost edge of town. Crumbling and full of potholes, it marked the official town limit—and the beginning of a natural paradise.

Taking the road south a short distance, they again turned east, traversing a narrow swath of woods which quickly gave rise to Silver Hills (named for its abundant population of silver maple trees; on windy days, the entire hillside springs to life in waves of silvery swirls).

Climbing up Silver Hills, they eventually came to a clearing at the top, where Hope Creek ran through a deep canyon below. The steep rocky walls shot straight downward, forming a natural barrier to would-be travelers and hikers—and especially young, eager hunters.

Sometime forever ago, the early townsfolk had constructed a rope bridge across the canyon. Looping heavy, stout rope through thick planks of sturdy oak, they lashed it to anchors planted deep into the rock on either side of the canyon, stretching it across the narrowest point available, where Old Rope dangles high above the creek to this day.

Of course, today there are modern bridges all throughout Hope, stitching the town back together where Hope Creek cuts through as it takes a quick southeastern jaunt through town before turning south again just north of Silver Hills—including a new six-lane steel monstrosity up on the northwest side of town where the highway goes across.

But up there in Silver Hills—where abundant wilderness begs to be explored, and has yet to be conquered—Old Rope is still the only way to cross Hope Creek Canyon.

On the other side of the dangling rope bridge, a huge open field sprawled, offering fertile hunting grounds for any young, ambitious hunters who just happened to be off school for the summer and were excruciatingly bored and needed something to do, preferably out of the house and away from nosy parents.

The back of the field ended at a nearly solid wall of trees, the forest known in town as Black Woods. The dense, spooky woods was the source of many legends and mysteries that have haunted the town for generations; eerie folklore recounted so convincingly by the old-timers around town that it worried the parents, spooked the teenagers, and scared the total bejeebers out of the kids.

And, right in front of Black Woods, a huge, ancient oak tree stood alone in the field, like a sentinel, a gatekeeper, towering over the boys as they hunted their prey. It almost seemed that in order to pass into the woods—which few dared do anyway—

one would have to first gain permission from that massive oak standing guard at the entrance.

Behind that oak, the thick woods that blanketed the east side of Silver Hills were so dark, foggy, and ominous—even said to be impenetrable in some places—that the entire forest was shrouded in mystery.

And frightening stories abounded; you name it—monsters, aliens, giant wild animals, serial killers, wood dwellers, witches, ghosts, evil spirits, whatever—it had probably inhabited those evil Black Woods at some time or another, wreaking havoc on the townsfolk—and especially anyone who dared even pass near, let alone venture in.

And all these various inhabitants had been blamed for all sorts of mysterious events and tragedies over the years; strange sightings near the woods, occult-like artifacts discovered anywhere in the area or even in town, glowing lights in or above the woods at night, UFOs, weird, unexplained sounds drifting from the woods, pets suffering mysteriously injuries as if ferociously attacked, etc.

But the most popular of all were the various tales of strange and unexplained disappearances—missing pets for one (but who knows really), and even the occasional vanishing adult, especially the elderly (but then again, any of those folks could have simply left town without telling anyone, or, if senile or suffering dementia, without even knowing they were doing so. It happens).

But the one mystery that truly goes unexplained is that of the children who have gone missing over the years without a trace. The town's history was peppered with such reports, going back decades.

The mystery of the vanishing children has become the talk of the town (though generally considered rather taboo most of the time; everyone avoided discussing it, and even if they did, they did so quietly, whispering under their breath).

But there's one thing that everyone agrees on, and is always mentioned whenever the subject comes up: that at night, out in Black Woods, the missing children can be heard screaming in the distance, seemingly coming from all directions at once, yet none discernible.

This collective wailing is rumored to be the ghosts of the missing children, forever haunting the dark, eerie, mysterious woods that lurk on the back of Silver Hills, over on the other side of Hope Creek Canyon.

Some people even say that the woods themselves are evil.

But everyone.agrees: there are strange goings on up there in Black Woods, and it's best to keep a good distance away.

•

So today, the boys casually crossed Old Rope (there was no wind, so *no problema*) and ventured into the dangerous hunting grounds on the other side of the creek, just like they had done countless times since *The Acquisition*.

Their mission (oh, and you better believe they chose to accept it):

1. Bring order to the world of the untamed;

2. Bring justice to the enemy;

3. Show everyone who was boss;

4. Generally wreak havoc on the lives of any unfortunate creatures—be they fowl, rodentia, or reptilian—that happened to cross their path or carelessly reveal its hiding place.

And they fully intended to accomplish their mission, come hell or high water (and hopefully before they got hungry and were forced to abandon their mission, heading quickly back to Winnie's house for *beanie-weenies*).

They thought if they were lucky, maybe one day they'd get

a shot at the cotton-ball end of a jackrabbit as it ricocheted back and forth ahead of them before disappearing into the brush as quickly as it had burst before them; but so far, no score. It was their dream to bag one of those *waskowy wabbits* someday, and the boys had a running bet as to which of them would be the first to do so.

But success had eluded them all month, despite their new weapons. During their countless missions, they hadn't scored a single hit—no mouse, no rat, no chipmunk, no squirrel, no bird, no snake—no *nothing*.

And they hadn't even *seen* a rabbit.

And today, it was more of the same. Nothing. By noon, all they'd succeeded in doing, really, was scattering hundreds of hardened steel ball-bearings surreptitiously into the ground all throughout the currently undeveloped field.

Perhaps one day, long into the future, some of that secretly planted ammo would finally serve its initial purpose of damage infliction—not via penetration of fur or feather, however, but through the vicious pinging assault of some hapless new home-owner's lawnmower blade.

The metallic ambush would inevitably cause a swearing middle-aged man to miss the first quarter of the game while he dashed off to the hardware store to secure a new blade so he could get the hell back, finish the damn yard, turn on the game, and start the beer.

After crossing Old Rope, the boys had ventured eastward across the front side of the field, then back again, shooting at random targets, but none of the living variety. Nearing the bridge on their return trip, they stopped, peering out across the field toward Black Woods.

"You wanna try the back side of the field?" Winnie asked.

"Yeah, why not. Maybe there's somethin over there, since

it's closer to the woods. But first I wanna check my ammo, I think I'm gettin low."

As Winnie watched, Tommy flipped his Wrist-Wrocket over and unscrewed the cap from the bottom of the handle. He was shocked—not a single ball bearing rolled out.

Empty.

How could this be?

Situation Critical...

He summoned his commander voice: "I seem to be out of ammunition—do you have any extra, Commander Winston?"

Winnie unscrewed his handle, and they watched as only two balls rolled out into his hand.

"Last two, then I'm out, Commander Thomas."

He palmed one and handed the other one over.

Desperate, they double-checked all their pockets, plunging and patting themselves all over—but came up empty. Realizing the futility of their situation, they stared earnestly at one another, each hoping the other would think of something.

Tommy shrugged. "C'mon, let's head back to base—maybe we'll see somethin on the way," he suggested.

"Yeah," Winnie agreed. "I'm gettin hungry anyways."

Hearts sinking, they started back to Command Base One.

"After lunch we can ride to Hank's and get more ammo."

"Yeah."

They crunched across the field toward the bridge, swinging their empty slingshots at the fluffy dandelion tufts along the way. Swarms of white seeds filled the air around them like tiny paratroopers, swirling wildly about before slowly floating off to explore new lands.

Upon descending Silver Hills, they stepped side-by-side from the woods out onto the old unnamed road. There, they stood in silence for a moment, looking to the south, where the road curved around to the west. A large, vacant, triangular lot sat inside that curve, covered in wild grass, a line of trees running along its back side.

"There it is." Winnie announced with a smile.

"Yep." Tommy concurred with his own smile.

"The very field where you homered on that asshole Eric Brunes...can't believe that was a year ago already."

"Yeah...a whole year, and he's still an asshole!"

They both laughed, then headed towards Winnie's house, reminiscing about Tommy's very first home run...

•

When Tommy smacked that baseball clear out of the field —to all his friend's astonishment, and even his own—it wasn't an easy pitch, or blind luck, or even divine intervention.

No, Tommy had *practiced.*

The spring after Tommy's fifth-grade year, when he was eleven, he decided he was going to learn to hit, come hell or high water. He was tired of striking out and being made fun of, every single time he played with the neighborhood kids in a pickup game.

So, the very first Saturday after school let out, he got started. Got up early, got dressed, and, with ball and bat in hand, took off out the back door of their farmhouse and headed for the back forty. He tromped through the uncut grass and knee-high weeds all the way out to the old dilapidated barn that leaned precariously to one side just inside the rear fence line, where his dad kept all sorts of old farm equipment and other crap he never used anymore but was afraid to get rid of.

He was going to put that old barn to good use for once; as of today, he had re-commissioned it as his rebound backboard for batting practice.

Standing some twenty feet from the barn, he tossed the ball, swung, and missed. Tossed the ball, swung, and missed.

When his older brother Will found out what he was doing, he thought he was nuts.

"That's never gonna work," he chided. "In *real* baseball, the ball is *pitched*. You'll never learn to hit it right by tossing it to *yourself*, dipshit."

Of course, Will would never in a million years volunteer to pitch to him, and Tommy knew better than to ask. There's no way he'd do it—especially if there was any chance any of his friends might see them playing together.

And besides, even if he *did* agree to do it, he'd probably just end up throwing the ball *at* him, instead of pitching it *to* him, and he was a pretty good shot, and could throw really hard, and Tommy wasn't about to take that chance. He knew better.

Will was a mean kid, a bully—just like their dad.

And of course he wasn't about to ask his dad, either. Especially in the middle of a binge. His binges came and went, but in the middle, when they peaked, the reeking half-dressed man carried the bottle around with him everywhere he staggered, alternating between fits of rage and bouts of sleep that bordered on unconsciousness. He didn't go anywhere—not even to the bathroom—without that seemingly unemptyable bottle clutched in one hand, the brown liquid sloshing.

And about the time Tommy had decided to start practicing out at the barn, was right about the time his old man was carrying the bottle around. Not a good time to ask—or say—*anything*. Tommy knew from experience that just as his father's clenched fist could bring that bottle to his lips, his other fist could just as easily be brought to Tommy's. And worse, he'd be grounded in the house at least a week, to reduce the risk of anyone seeing his cuts and bruises before they healed, then asking questions or making phone calls or otherwise butting into old man Baker's private affairs.

And Tommy wasn't sure which was worse—the beatings, or the groundings—and had no desire to run any experiments to find out.

So he figured he would just have to learn to hit on his own.

Toss, swing, miss. Toss, swing, miss...

After a few dozen tosses, he started occasionally making contact, tipping one behind him or ricocheting it straight into the ground; after a few hundred, he actually started catching some good, solid hits; after a few *thousand*, he was regularly hitting the ball, the *crack!* of the bat and the *thwack!* of the ball striking the wooden slats on the side of the old barn echoing off into the woods behind the property.

Before long, it was getting pretty easy, so he decided to up the challenge a bit: he began throwing the ball up on the top of the barn and waiting as it bounced haphazardly around on the slanted roof, then dropped down in a totally random place, at a totally random speed.

He learned to quickly gauge the ball as it fell from the edge; and though he only had a second or two to do so, over time he got pretty good at it, successfully hitting the ball more often than not.

And that's what he did. Day after day, toss after toss, swing after swing—for two solid weeks.

Will may have been right—that's not the way to learn to hit a *pitched* ball; but what Tommy did learn, without really even being aware of it, was even more important: *how to keep his eye on the ball.*

Then one Saturday, over at Winnie's house, while the two were lounging around out on the front porch reading and comparing comic books, a gaggle of neighborhood kids came riding by on their bikes, heading for the field down on the south end of The Flats for a pickup game. On their way past, Eric Brunes waved them in, and they readily abandoned their superheroes (the comic books were all old ones anyway), ran inside for their mitts, then jumped on their bikes and peddled ferociously down the street to join up with the gang.

They all parked their bikes on the edge of the street and flooded onto the field. It was a vacant lot, overgrown with wild grass, which the kids had converted into a makeshift ball diamond a few summers ago, using square pieces of plywood for bases, which they stashed in the tree line behind the field for safe keeping.

After retrieving the wooden bases from hiding and placing them around the diamond, the kids divvied up teams, flipped a coin—and Tommy's team got first bat.

Eric was pitching for the other team (he was a year older, half a foot taller, and a lot stronger (and meaner) than the rest of them, so he always pitched, nobody argued this).

Danny Leer was first up, a decent player, could hit okay, and after one strike he caught one, good connection—but it went straight into the mitt of Chris McDaniels at short stop.

Winnie was up next. A skinny kid with thick glasses and a pale, freckled complexion, with fine, dark hair that was cut into straight bangs across his forehead—almost a bowl cut, with his small jug-ears sticking out on each side—he was not, by any stretch of the imagination, an athlete. So he looked somewhat comical, standing there intently holding a bat up in the air that was thicker than his own arms.

As usual, Eric easily struck him out, burning three fast balls in a row right by him. Winnie whiffed them all, swinging at the last one so hard his glasses tumbled off and landed right in the middle of home plate, prompting laughing and heckling from both teams as he timidly retrieved them and slumped away.

Then it was Tommy's turn to bat. He stood poised at the plate, bat held high, exactly as he had practiced thousands of times over the past two weeks, ready for the ball to come down crazy and unpredictable from the barn roof.

Knowing that Tommy couldn't hit—he usually whiffed it, just like Winnie—Eric made the mistake of thinking this would be an easy out. So for show, and probably more just to make Tommy look foolish, Eric performed a wide variety of crazy, gesticulated antics during his windup—prompting laughter from the kids on both teams—then, stepping forward, he at first feigned another fast ball—but at the last second held up and instead tossed a high, slow floater toward Tommy.

The ball sailed in high above Tommy's head, then suddenly dropped in front of him just as it reached the plate (pretty much just as it did during his practice sessions).

Keeping his eye on the ball, gauging its speed and distance as it dropped, Tommy swung with everything he had.

CRACK!

The solid impact of bat against ball was so loud and unexpected—sounded like a firecracker going off—that many of his teammates behind him actually flinched.

But Tommy just stood in disbelief as he watched the ball sail well over everyone's head and into the bright summer sky. Spencer Lewis—who was the youngest and smallest kid in the group, so was always stationed out at center field because nobody could usually hit the ball that far anyway—turned and ran across the outfield as the ball sailed over him and toward the trees in the back.

Running as fast as he could, but to no avail, at the last second he threw his mitt into the air in futility as the ball fell and disappeared into the trees, thumping and cracking its way to the ground somewhere unseen.

Incredulous, Tommy proudly trotted the bases, his team-mates screaming and cheering. As he crossed home, they all crowded around him, cheering and patting him on the back and congratulating him on the most awesome homer they'd ever seen.

In the middle of all the ruckus, Tommy heard Eric shout from behind him, "Hey asshole!"

Tommy turned to find Eric staring down at him, pointing his finger in his face.

"Nobody *ever* homers on me!" He barked. *"EVER!"*

With that, he turned as if to walk away—but then stopped, leaned slightly onto one leg...and launched a round-house.

And Tommy never saw it coming; suddenly, he both felt and heard the stinging explosion of Eric's fist as it met his face. Spinning violently, he landed face-down in the dirt

suddenly, he both felt and heard the stinging explosion of the back of his father's hand as it met his face. Spinning violently, he landed face-down on the hardwood floor.

Arms and legs outstretched, he slid across the smooth floor toward the small bookcase that sat under his bedroom window, his wood desk chair tumbling away behind him to stop against the bed.

Rolling painfully over, he saw his dad standing over him, pointing his finger at his face.

"Don't you ever talk back to me!" he barked. "EVER!"

With that he took a swig from the ever-present bottle.

Tommy blinked up at him, wiping the blood from his swelling lips and right nostril. He hadn't talked back, really—he'd merely made an observation. But either way, he should have known better than to say anything at all when his old man was on a binge. During those times, It didn't matter much what he did, what he said—his dad was just as likely to start talking hand to him anyway, soon as something set him off. And just about any little thing could set him off.

This time, he'd been sitting quietly at his desk in his bedroom, minding his own business, engrossed in the novel Treasure Island, his fifth-grade reading assignment, when his dad had suddenly appeared in the doorway.

Tommy ignored him, kept his nose in the book.

After looking around the room, he slurred:

"Make sure you clean up this dump fore you go to bed."

Tommy just kept on reading, afraid to speak. Staying under the radar.

Taking a swig, his father finally turned and disappeared down the hallway, prompting a sigh of relief from Tommy.

But a moment later, he was back. This time, he stepped fully into the room, now only a few feet from the boy's desk, looking down at him with contempt.

"You ignorin me?"

A swig.

"No sir," Tommy said, not looking up from the book.

"Sure looks like you're ignorin me."

"No, you're just drunk," he mumbled under his breath.

A surge of adrenaline coursed through him when he realized what he'd just said. He couldn't believe it. Sometimes he suspected there was a trap door between his brain and his mouth, the way stuff just tumbled out like that. Staring down at the book, he hoped the remark would slip by unnoticed. Or with any luck, maybe his dad hadn't even heard it.

Two quick steps toward him, just enough time for Tommy to turn and look up, a quick backhand, and now he was on the floor bleeding.

Again.

Funny, though—all he could think about was how he hoped

he didn't get any blood on the book, since it was from the school library and he'd probably be in trouble if he did

as the ruckus of shouting and cheering kids immediately stopped, replaced instead by a morbid silence that quickly spread across the ball field.

Reeling in pain, both hands clenched to his face, Tommy turned over to see Eric standing over him, face flush with anger. Turning, he made as if to leave—walking nonchalantly past Tommy as he writhed in the dirt—but suddenly turned and kicked him, hard, in the ribs. Tommy curled up in a ball, the wind knocked out of him.

Eric turned and stormed off, all the kids stepping out of his way as he barreled through the crowd. Hands shoved into his pockets, mitt clasped under one arm, and not once bothering to look back at the rest of them, he marched to his bike, mounted, and peddled away down the road.

Gasping for air, Tommy watched him go though the drifting clouds of dust, and couldn't help but wonder if Eric's dad carried a bottle around sometimes, too.

Once the bully had turned the corner and was gone, the rest of the group gathered around and helped Tommy off the ground, murmuring their condolences and spewing profanities about Eric.

Tommy brushed himself off, wiped at his bloody nose with his shirttail. The bleeding was already stopping, and the pain in his ribs was already subsiding, and when he finally began regaining his breath, he knew he'd be okay.

After stashing the plywood bases back in the tree line, the kids all rode to Spencer's house, because his mom usually made homemade ice cream—and sure enough, there was plenty for them to indulge.

Soon Eric Brunes and his stupid temper tantrum were

forgotten—but the legend of Tommy's awesome homer would live on forever.

Tommy may have spent a few weeks that spring learning how to hit—but in those few short minutes after hitting that homer, he learned quite a bit about life.

•

After lunch (double-decker peanut butter and jelly sandwiches, groovy potato chips, and Dr Pepper), the boys pretended to watch TV while they waited for Winnie's mom to leave for work. When she finally kissed her son goodbye (which, embarrassed, he made a show of rubbing off in disgust after she left the room), they waited for her car to turn the corner at the end of Hillsboro Lane. When she was finally out of view, they ran outside, jumped on their bikes, and headed for town.

When they finally pushed into the cool air conditioning and bright fluorescent lighting of Hank's Hobbies & Sporting Gear, they couldn't believe their luck: Hank was there again!

They bolted to the counter, where Hank stood with his back to them, clipboard in one hand, jabbing a pen across the items on the shelves with the other, apparently counting stuff.

"Hey, Hank!" the boys greeted in unison.

Hank turned around—but instead of looking bright-eyed and peppy like he usually did, he looked rather perturbed, frowning, mouth turned down slightly at the corners.

"How's it goin kids?" he said quietly, setting his clipboard and pen down and leaning with both hands on the counter.

"What's up?"

Still not smiling, he looked solemnly down at them, waiting, almost like they were bothering him.

"Um...we just need to get another box of balls for our Wrist-Wrockets," Tommy said.

"Two boxes," Winnie interjected.

"Yeah, two boxes—one each."

Hank sighed, turned around, looked around on the shelves, snatched two white boxes down, then turned and tossed them rather roughly onto the counter before them. The boys turned and looked at each other, wondering why he was acting this way, when he was usually so cheerful and fun to be around.

"Two boxes of balls. Anything else?"

"No sir, that'll do it." Tommy answered.

As Hank was ringing them up, Winnie remembered about the deal they got before, and piped up: "Hey—can you give us a deal, like last time? Like buy two get one free or something?"

Tommy looked from Winnie back to Hank, hopeful.

"Yeah, you got any deals goin today?"

Hank sighed again, stopped ringing, and just stood glaring down at them.

"You know, you kids are a real piece of work," he grumbled.

The boys looked at each other again, perplexed, then back to Hank.

"I work hard, all day long, seven days a week, tryin to make a livin off this hole in the wall—"

—he waved his hand slowly over their heads, referencing the store behind them—

"—and most the time, I just get by. I do alright, but I ain't rollin, if you know what I mean. And sure, I don't mind helpin you kids out once in awhile, I know you got it hard too—but damned if y'all don't come in here always wantin free shit now! This stuff don't grow on trees, ya know."

Winnie looked at the floor, embarrassed, and Tommy's eyes widened, apologetic.

"Gee, sorry Hank," he apologized. "That's okay, don't worry about it—we don't need a discount or anything for free, just thought we'd ask is all."

Without another word, Hank rang up the balls.

"That'll be eight thirty-eight."

The boys dug in their pockets, pooled their money, then slid eight crumpled bills and two quarters across the counter.

He snatched them up, flung the register open, slapped them in, dug the change out, and slammed the drawer shut.

"Twelve cents," he muttered as he flippantly tossed the coins into Tommy's outstretched hand. Pulling a white plastic bag from behind the counter somewhere, he stuffed the two boxes and the receipt into it and handed it over.

"There ya are."

They both mumbled thank yous as Tommy dragged the bag off the counter, and they turned and headed for the door, walking rather quickly to get out of there. But halfway to the door, Hank called them back, his voice softening a bit.

"Hey, kids, wait a sec. Come back over here."

They stopped and looked at each other for a moment, then walked slowly back to the counter, wondering what to expect. Hank was obviously in a bad mood today, and they didn't want to get scolded again.

As they approached him, Hank leaned his hand over the counter, motioning for Tommy to surrender the bag.

Tommy handed it up to him, and he set it on the counter, opened the top, turned, grabbed two more boxes of balls, then turned back and dropped them into the bag with the first two.

"Sorry I talked to you that way," he said as he was tying the top of the bag. "Havin a bad day, that's all. Didn't mean to take it out on you guys."

He handed the bag back to Tommy.

"There. Buy two, get two. And I appreciate your business."

Now he was smiling.

The boys' faces lit up.

"Gee, thanks Hank!" they shouted in unison.

"Now get outta here," he motion to the door with a jerk of his chin. "You boys have fun with those Wrist-Wrockets—and be careful!"

The boys thanked him again and bounced toward the door, suddenly feeling on top of the world.

On their way out the door, Hank shouted after them: "And try to stay cool out there, ya hear?"

"Okay!" they chimed in unison as they left the store.

"That was awesome!" Winnie said as they approached their bikes, again parked in the shade under the awning.

"Yeah, Hank's pretty cool. But I wonder what was up? I've never seen him act that way before."

Winnie shrugged. "Me neither."

"Somethin scared him this mornin," someone said, the voice coming from behind them.

The boys stopped under the awning and looked over at the end of the building, where the voice had come from. It was Joey—Hank's son—leaning against the wall, just around the corner, smoking, out of view of the front door. When the boys left the store, they'd walked right by him.

"What?" Tommy asked, surprised to see him there.

Joey flicked the butt onto the sidewalk in front of him and snuffed it out with his foot as he walked up to join them under the awning.

Leaning close, he spoke quietly.

"He's actin all weird like that cuz he saw somethin this mornin, when he was out fishin. Scared him pretty bad I think. He doesn't wanna talk about it, but it was bad enough he quit fishin early and came back. Said he needed to do inventory anyway—which I thought was odd, we usually do inventory the last day of the month—and he's been actin spooked all day."

"Really?" Tommy asked. "What'd he see?"

Joey shrugged. "Don't know. Like I said, he wont talk much about it. A few things, but no details really."

"Where was he fishin?" Winnie asked.

"You ain't gonna believe it," Joey said. He looked around to make sure nobody was within earshot, then leaned back in.

"Blackwater."

The boys' eyes widened.

"No way!" Tommy said, incredulous. "Everyone says to stay away from there, it's dangerous."

"Yeah," Winnie concurred. "That's the worst part of Black Woods—the *scariest* part—nobody goes in there!"

Blackwater was basically a big swamp. Down south of Hope Creek Canyon, on the southern end of Silver Hills where the creek emptied out of the canyon then turned and headed off to the southeast, there was a wide, low-lying area back at the tail end of Black Woods, that filled up whenever the creek crested after heavy rain or snow melt off. It was always flooded back in there, and since it was at the back side of Black Woods, everyone called it Blackwater.

And true to it's name, it was a dark and spooky swamp; a haven for wild animals, insects, parasites, you name it. And the water was always stagnant, sitting there for weeks or months at a time with little or no circulation, and feared to be full of bacteria and crap that could make you pretty sick. The kids were all warned to stay the hell away from it.

And they did.

"Yeah, well...he usually fishes south of there, where the creek bends back to the east. There's like a big pond there at the bend, shallow along the banks, lots of rocks and boulders, not much current, big shade trees all around. Usually does pretty good there, but not lately—like all summer, really, he hasn't caught shit—so, he worked it north, all the way up to Blackwater, then decided to go on in, try it out. Figured bein so shallow, and all that shade of the woods, nice and quiet, and nobody ever fishes there, should be hoppin with fish. And 'sides, he don't buy the stories anyhow, says they're all BS."

"Even the screaming kids?" Winnie asked. "The ones they say can be heard at night all around Black Woods, supposed to be the ghosts of all those missing kids over the years?"

"That? You don't believe that shit, do you?" Joey chuckled.

Winnie shrugged. "It's just what everyone says."

"My old man says yeah, you can hear what sounds like kids screamin out there, especially at night—but it's just the wind howling through the canyon, it ain't no ghosts of kids. It ain't no ghosts at all, cuz there's no such thing as ghosts, dumbass."

Winnie looked down, embarrassed. "Well, I still can't be-lieve he went in there."

"So what did he see? What scared him?" Tommy asked.

Joey looked behind him, toward the store window. Decid-ing his dad wasn't looking, he continued.

"Don't really know. All he said was he took the boat in as far as he could, but the water got real shallow and there were too many trees, so he tied it up, put his waders on, and started walkin. Picked a spot close to one bank, and started casting. But after awhile, he started hearing somethin, in the woods behind him."

The boys were riveted. But Joey took his time, milking it. Tapped out another cigarette, lit it. Looked around.

"C'mon! So what did he hear?" Winnie urged, unable to take the suspense any longer.

"Well, that's just it—he don't know. Said it sounded like somethin big, movin around on the bank. He kept lookin, but couldn't see nothin. Just a branch movin here or there, a bush rustlin. And once, there was a pretty loud *pop!*, and a flock of sparrows got spooked out of a tree, burst out over him, chirpin like the devil. But he said it was too dark back there on the bank, the woods are way too thick there, so he never did see whatever it was."

He took a drag, tilted his head back, blew a thin line of blue-gray smoke into the air above him, then continued.

"So he started gettin spooked, and decided to move somewhere else. Down the bank a little ways, further out from the woods. But didn't matter, this thing just kept followin him. He could hear it, said he could even *feel* it getting closer. He finally decided that whatever it was, it was stalking him, that was for sure."

Winnie let out a low whistle.

"So he never saw what it was? An Animal? Monster? Just somebody followin him? What?" Tommy pushed.

Joey shrugged. "He won't say. Says he never did see what it was. But y'ask me, I think he really *did* see it, whatever it was, he just don't wanna admit it, cuz he don't wanna talk about it. All he'll tell me is once he figured out it was stalkin him, he boogied back to the boat and got the fuck outta there."

"Damn," Tommy said. I wonder what it was?"

Joey shrugged. "May never know. But whatever it was, I think it really scared him. Pretty bad, too. I never seen him act like that before. And he won't talk about it, even to me. But he's like that—he don't talk about stuff that makes him uncomfortable—and there ain't much that makes him uncomfortable, at least that I know of."

As Joey took another drag, Tommy and Winnie looked at each other.

"You thinkin what I'm thinkin?" Tommy said.

"The shack." Winnie answered.

"Yeah. Maybe whoever—or whatever—is livin there is what Hank saw—or heard—stalkin him."

"Maybe." Winnie nodded.

"Shack? What shack? What the fuck are you two dweebs talkin about?" Joey interrupted.

"Well, a few days ago, I—" Tommy started, but Winnie quickly interrupted him.

"Hey—you're not gonna tell him, are ya? I thought we were keepin it secret."

"Keepin *what* secret?" Joey demanded, looking quickly back and forth between them. "Now you *gotta* tell me."

Tommy sighed, looking at the ground. "I don't know..."

Joey flicked his cigarette out into the street, then crossed his arms, towering over them menacingly.

"Okay, how about I kick both your asses unless you tell me?"

Tommy looked at Winnie.

"They'll probably find it anyway," he reasoned. "Since Hank thinks somethin's out there, they'll probably get some guys together and go huntin for it, like they usually do. And if they find it, or find its tracks and follow it, they'll probably find the shack, too. So it won't really matter, we might as well tell him."

Winnie nodded quietly in agreement.

"You guys got two seconds to start talkin, or I start swingin."

Tommy looked back at Joey, took a breath, and exhaled.

"Okay. A few days ago, I saw an old shack sittin way back in the woods behind this hidden cove off Hope Creek, at the last bend before the Canyon. So next day, me and Winnie went back out there to check it out..."

•

"I'm tellin you, it was there," Tommy said. "I *saw* it."

"And *I'm* tellin *you*, you're crazy, Winnie responded. "You were either just seeing things, or high—or both."

Leaving the end of railroad trestle, they skittered down the embankment toward the creek, scattering loose rocks about.

"I wasn't high. I told you: I swiped this pack of cigarettes from my old man's dresser yesterday, then came out here and took the boat out on the creek looking for a secluded spot somewhere to have a smoke. Then I thought of that cove we saw a few weeks ago—remember?"

"Yeah, I remember. Down a ways, at that bend, on the left."

"That's right, but we only saw it from out on the creek, we didn't go in. We weren't even sure it was really a cove, with all the branches and stuff in the way. But I thought if it *was*, it'd be a perfect hiding spot, so I went to take a look. And I was right—it's a most excellent hiding place...but while I was sittin back in there, I saw it, way back in the woods."

At the bottom of the embankment the ground flattened, the dirt becoming less rocky and more sandy. Turning together, the two approached the rotting wood pier that jutted out a short distance into the river. No longer in use, the old relic was almost entirely obscured by an overgrowth of brush and weeds that had re-claimed the land, creeping out from the woods behind to cloak the pier in a shroud of camouflage along both sides, extending almost to the water's edge.

The pier's outboard posts had sunk into the muddy river bottom long ago, so the whole thing ran out at a pronounced incline for about ten feet before disappearing under the murky brown water.

Underneath, a small aluminum rowboat lay upside down, all but hidden from view.

Without a word, the boys split up, each stepping around opposite ends of the overgrowth and taking positions at each end of the overturned boat. In unison, they bent and hooked their hands under the dirty aluminum edge.

"Watch for snakes."

"Yep."

Together, they pulled the boat out from under the pier, cocked it at a slight angle, then dragged it over the weeds and brush until they had room to flop it over on an open patch of ground between the pier and the creek.

They'd done it so many times, they now had it down: once they'd traveled back just so far, they stopped simultaneously, lifted the side of the boat to shoulder height, then flopped it over onto the sandy ground with a *thunk!*

They scanned the boat's interior carefully as it rocked back and forth before finally settling.

No snakes.

"Remember that one time last summer, that snake came crawlin out from under the seat? Pete about shit."

They both chuckled.

"Yeah, scared him so bad he jumped back and fell on his ass in the water."

Smiling with the memory, they walked back to the pier, crouched behind the weeds, and fetched the oars out of the darkness underneath. Carrying one each, they turned and walked together back to the boat.

"And it was just a water snake—but now he won't even come down here anymore."

"Well, yeah—cuz of his old man."

"Oh, yeah, that's right...almost forgot about that."

While Pete's family was camping out west a few years back, his dad was bit by a snake—a Diamondback, one of the most lethal—and nearly died. Fortunately, in preparation for the trip, the entire family had taken a first aid training course together—and their quick action was credited with saving the man's life. But he'd been laid up in the hospital for days, and for awhile they didn't know if he was going to make it. Eventually, he pulled through—but now Pete was deathly afraid of all snakes, poisonous or not.

After laying the oars in the boat, one along each side, the boys stepped to the rear of the boat, bent, and pushed it toward the water, the hull moaning loudly as it scraped across a scattering of rocks imbedded in the mud. The moaning suddenly stopped as the boat glided gently onto the water, and they took turns hopping in.

As if by silent command, they took their usual positions: Tommy to the front seat, Winnie to the rear. Once the boat stopped rocking, they dropped their oars, one to each side, and guided the boat expertly out onto the quiet water.

They were on the northeast side of town, a large expanse of largely undeveloped land, acres and acres of rolling fields interrupted occasionally with narrow swaths of woods, a sparsely populated area of town known to the locals as The Meadows. The western edge of The Meadows is marked by the old, rusty steel trestle that took the railroad tracks over Hope Creek to continue north.

Starting at Winnie's house in The Flats, they could walk the train tracks all the way up to The Meadows, cross over the creek via the trestle, then descend to the creek below to the abandoned pier.

Last summer, when they had first discovered the pier, they were ecstatic at finding the boat underneath. They pulled it out, tested it for leaks, and have been using it ever since, unsure of who, if anyone, it belonged to. But every time they came back, here it was, just as they'd left it, under the old pier and camouflaged by the surrounding foliage.

From the pier, they could take the boat down Hope Creek all the way around to the east side of town, then turn back around before Silver Hills began, where the banks on both sides of the creek suddenly began rising, eventually creating Hope Creek Canyon.

They didn't dare risk going in; there would be no way out until the other end, and there were jutting ledges, sharp turns, rapids, and boulders all along the way.

At least that's what they'd heard anyway.

So no, they were careful to turn around as soon as they saw the banks rising, the emerging rock faces glaring menacingly out at them.

It hadn't rained much lately, so today the creek was moving so slowly it seemed deceptively motionless; but once they got the boat pointed downstream, it continued steadily on its own, they just had to guide it a little with their oars.

As they cleared the first bend and the creek turned south, they immediately took advantage of the seclusion: Tommy pulled the stolen pack of cigarettes from his shirt pocket, shook one to the top, plucked it out with his lips, then shook out another and offered it up to Winnie, who reached out, slid it out, and placed it to his lips.

Tommy then returned the pack to his shirt pocket, pulled a lighter from the back pocket of his jeans, lit up, and handed it to his friend.

Once they were both lit, they relaxed in silence, just smoking and drifting. As they pretended to inhale, a new demeanor overtook them—an older look, a stronger, more confident look.

Suddenly, they were no longer boys; they were men now.

As they drifted in silence, Winnie threw his head back and blew a thin stream of smoke into the air. Watching the smoke dissipate above, he said to the sky:

"I still don't believe you."

"You'll see."

Cigarette dangling from his lips, Tommy turned and began paddling.

•

Before long they saw the cove approaching on the left, in the last bend before Silver Hills began to rise and the creek flowed into the canyon.

Dense woods huddled right up to the bank there, and the entire cove was shrouded in long, overhanging tree branches that drooped all the way to the river's surface, effectively camouflaging the entrance. If you didn't know it was there, you'd float right past and never see it. It was only blind luck that they'd spotted it a few weeks earlier—and that was just because they were watching a turtle swimming along the bank, its head poking up out of the water, when it turned and disappeared under the branches and into the cove.

Flicking their butts out into the river, they both turned and began paddling the boat toward the nearly hidden cove, then stopped and let their momentum carry them the rest of the way in, the boat gliding silently on the still water. Tommy reached forward with his oar, lifting a large Sycamore branch up, its broad leaves wet and dripping. As he did so, Winnie paddled from the rear, and they slipped effortlessly under.

When the big Sycamore branch came down behind them, they were completely enclosed by the overhanging branches behind, and the dense foliage crowding the bank around them.

Winnie let out a long, admiring whistle.

"Damn...this is nice."

"Tolja."

They looked around for a moment, then continued inward, occasionally ducking low branches. The cove cut into the bank about twenty feet, then hooked back to the left. Once they rounded the turn, the water was shallow enough they could reach the bottom with their oars. Shoving their oars into the gravel underneath, they walked the boat into the back leg of the cove—now just wide enough for the boat, not much wider —until they bottomed out against the bank.

Tommy's head bobbed and weaved as he peered through the woods in front of them, looking for it.

"There!" He pointed deep into the woods.

Winnie tried to follow his arm, peering into the trees.

"I don't see anything."

"See that big oak back there? Look to the left of that, there's a small opening in the pines, and you can see way back there."

Winnie did as instructed, but shrugged.

"I still don't see anything."

"It's behind the pines. See the line of pines back there?"

Winnie squinted deep into the woods, bobbing his head as he tried to see past all the obstructions.

"Okay, I see the pines, I think."

"Keep looking. You'll see it. Just past the pines, through that little opening in the middle. It's dark, so it's kinda hard to see. Keep looking. Let your eyes adjust for a second."

Suddenly, Winnie's eyes widened.

"There it is! I see it! So you weren't just seeing things!"

"Tolja."

Abandoning their oars in the boat, they stepped out together onto the bank.

•

Hands on hips, they stood quietly together looking at the old, dilapidated shack. It was small, maybe twenty feet square, and made entirely of wood—warped and split wood slats running along all sides, cracked and rotted wood shingles on the roof, a few missing. And all the wood surfaces were blackened with age, with decay.

The entire structure appeared to be hand-built, leaning slightly to one side, with every expanse of wall or roof bowing downward like an old swaybacked horse, threatening collapse.

Each of the three visible walls contained one small square window, all of which were broken, exposing ratty cloths hanging inside, makeshift curtains. In the front, the door was also made of thin, rotted wood, split and splintered and blackened. It stood ajar, pushed a foot or so inward from its warped frame, revealing a brief section of dirty wood floor which disappeared into darkness.

Winnie let out a low whistle.

"Do you think anyone lives here?" he whispered.

"Sure doesn't look like it, with the door open like that," Tommy said. "And all the windows are broken."

The boys crept first to one side of the shack, then around to the other, craning their necks trying to see into the darkness through the broken windows, listening for any sounds within.

"I sure don't hear anything," Tommy muttered.

"Me neither...but I don't know..."

Finally, Tommy crept up to the front of the shack, tip-toeing up onto the cracked and faded wood porch, doing his best to step quietly around all the dead, dry leaves. Winnie stayed behind, watching his friend from a distance.

Once he reached the doorway, he leaned in just far enough to peer around the door and into the darkness. After a moment, looking and listening, he turned back to Winnie and shrugged.

In response, Winnie ventured up onto the porch, stopping close behind Tommy.

"I don't think anyone's here." Tommy whispered.

Just then a breeze blew through the woods, rustling the trees around them and initiating a low, hollow moan as it coursed its way through the shack, pushing the tattered curtains inward from the glassless window frames, then exiting the open front door, blowing the dead leaves at their feet away across the front porch. The whole event reinforced the notion of emptiness within.

"Hello?" Tommy called through the door. "Anyone home?"

Nothing. Birds chirping, leaves rustling in the trees.

Looking at each other, they shrugged and shook their heads.

Tommy gently pushed the crumbling wooden door open, squeaking it back on rusty hinges. They both glanced around inside, then looked at each other again, shrugged again.

Then they ventured inside.

It was empty. A single large room, with one small square window on each wall except the back one, allowing just a bit of sunlight in. The floor was wood, but covered with dirt and leaves. The entire framework was exposed, the single-ply walls consisting of planks mounted to the outside, with no interior walls added. And no ceiling either, the room extending upward ten or twelve feet, angled on both sides by the roof, seams and holes glowing with sunlight. Spiderwebs and cobwebs occupied nearly every available corner, and the place stank of mold, rotted wood, and...something else...something gamey, like an animal's den or dog cage.

Stopping just inside the door, the boys looked around in the semi-darkness. Though there was no furniture, there *were* all sorts of odds and ends lying about, mostly along the walls, which at first glance appeared to simply be discarded trash. But upon closer inspection, almost all of it was dishes, or food-related: plastic cups, soiled and molding paper plates, fast-food and deli-food packages, open and discarded cans (beans, soup, corn, etc), plastic eating utensils, wadded napkins, empty to-go drink cups capped with lids and straws.

"Looks like someone's been living here," Tommy said.

"Or some *thing*, anyway," Winnie corrected.

At this, Tommy turned and looked at him.

"Well, it could be anything," Winnie explained, pushing his glasses up on his nose. "Could be a person—a homeless person, a crazy person, a hermit, who knows—or it could be an animal. Like raccoons. They dig in trash cans all the time. Or a mountain lion, or coyote, or even just a dog. Or maybe even a *monster*, like the one in all those stories they tell around town. *Anything* could be carrying food in here an eating it."

Tommy rolled his eyes.

"A monster. Eating fast food?" Tommy asked in an incredulous tone, pointing to an empty Big Mac container. "Fountain sodas with lids and straws? Plastic forks? And when's the last time you heard of a monster that used a can opener? Or an animal, for that matter?"

"Just sayin, jeez."

"No, whatever's been living here has to be smart enough to open tin cans, drink out of straws, and clean up with napkins. So either it's a person, or it's the smartest animal—"

"Or monster."

—it's not a monster!"

Looking around the room, Tommy spotted something in the corner, and headed over.

"See? Look right here," he said as approached the right rear corner of the room. There, he kicked around a pile of old clothing, rags, a tattered blanket, that was all lying there in an elongated fashion.

"Looks like a bed."

"Man, I didn't even *see* that, with all the trash. I bet it is."

They scanned around the room again, taking a closer look.

"What's that?" Winnie asked, pointing to the opposite, left rear corner of the room. "See that round black thing there in the other corner?"

The sun, at its southwest angle, was shining in from the front and right side of the shack, so the rear and left portions of the room were much darker. And with no window at all in the back wall, the left rear corner was the darkest of all.

"I don't know," Tommy said, walking over.

Winnie followed.

Closer now, they saw that the round black thing wasn't a *thing* at all—but a hole in the floor.

"No shit," Tommy said, pushing one toe into the hole, verifying there was nothing there but air and darkness.

About two feet wide, the opening ran right up against both walls, the hole disappearing down into the earth. Winnie shifted to the side, while Tommy stood in front, and they both crouched, hands on knees, peering down into the darkness.

"Can you see anything?" Winnie asked.

"No, it's too dark in here. I can't see shit."

They both stooped to their knees, hands gripping the edges of the flooring, looking in, trying to see something down there.

"I think I see the bottom," Tommy said. "Looks like it's about five or six feet deep, then goes back that way." As he described it, he pointed to the rear of the house.

With that, he hooked one hand on the ledge, and swung himself down into the hole.

"Hey, don't—!" Winnie began to protest, but it was too late.

Tommy landed in the soft dirt at the bottom with a *thump!,* stood and peered into the darkness for a moment, then turned and looked back up at Winnie.

"Looks like it goes back a ways, like a tunnel. I think I see light down at the other end, maybe twenty feet away. Thirty."

"Really? It's a tunnel out to the woods?" Winnie asked.

"Looks like it."

Winnie sat, dangled his feet into the hole, then dropped in. Turning, he examined the dirt wall behind him. Starting about halfway up, a series of divots were dug deeply into the dirt, stringy roots dangling from them.

"Look, they're like steps," Winnie said.

Tommy stepped closer, ran his hand into a few of the holes.

"Yep. For climbing back up into the shack."

"Uh-huh."

When they turned from the wall, they heard strange, hollow clacking sounds at their feet, and the both stopped to look —but it was too dark. Tommy knelt, feeling with his hands and straining to see. From this close, he could just make them out.

"Bones!"

Winnie knelt beside him, running his hands all around. There were dry, hollow bones everywhere, scattered around on the floor and piled all along the corners against walls.

"What kind do you think they are?" Winnie asked.

"Don't know. They're pretty small, probably too small to be human. So some kind of animal I guess."

"Weird. So whoever—or whatever—lives here hunts animals, brings them back here, eats them, then tosses the bones down here you think?"

Tommy shrugged. "Could be. Or maybe some animal—like you say, a mountain lion, a coyote, or even a dog—just uses this tunnel, comes in here and eats, where it's quiet and protected. Hard tellin, really."

They stood and peered down the long dirt tunnel. The far end glowed slightly where it opened back up into the woods.

"So, let's see where it goes," Tommy said, starting forward.

Winnie grabbed his arm. "I don't know...who knows what's down at the other end? What if it *is* an animal? And what if it's hangin out in the woods down on that end? Huntin or somethin? We just gonna walk up on it, like, hey there, Mr. Moun-tain Lion, how's it—"

—but he stopped short, as they heard a thump above them.

"What was tha—" Winnie started.

"Shhhh!" Tommy cut him off.

Another thump, some shuffling sounds.

"Somebody's up there!" Winnie whispered.

"Probably just the wind," Tommy whispered back.

Then the clang and rattle of an empty tin can hitting the floor, bouncing and rolling.

"Let's get out of here!" Tommy hissed, and they both darted down the tunnel toward the growing light at the other end.

That end was angled upward, and they were able to scam-per up the inclined wall on hands and knees, spewing dirt and pebbles behind them as they went. Bursting to the surface, they flopped themselves onto the ground among the trees some thirty feet or so behind the shack. To their relief, there were no wild animals lying in wait, ready to devour them; just a flock of sparrows, which burst from the tree above when they emerged from the tunnel, twittering away into the woods.

Crouching in the brush, they quietly peered at the shack, but didn't see or hear anything, or anyone.

Then Winnie had a thought; turning, he peered into the darkening woods behind them. His eyes widened as he turned back to Tommy.

"Hey—is this Black Woods?" he nervously whispered.

Tommy turned and looked for a moment, then shrugged.

"I don't think so. Black Woods is downstream a ways, up on the back of Silver Hills. Probably pretty close, though."

After a minute of silence, and they hadn't seen anything, Tommy signaled with an outstretched arm to go around the other way, far clear of the shack, to return to the boat. Winnie nodded in understanding. Remaining crouched, they slinked off through the woods, glancing at the shack as they circled it, but seeing nothing.

Back in the boat, they shoved off as quickly as they could, exited the cove, and started paddling upstream. It wasn't until they were far from the cove that they dared break their silence.

"So what do you think it was?" Winnie finally asked.

"Probably just the wind, like I said," Tommy answered with a shrug. "Wind came in through the broken windows, blew some stuff around. An empty can rolled across the floor."

"I don't know," Winnie was skeptical. "That can sounded like it was *tossed* onto the floor. I think whoever's living there— or *what* ever's living there—came back, and we're just lucky we were already down in that tunnel when it did."

Tommy fetched the pack of cigarettes, slid one out with his lips, offered the pack up to Winnie.

"I think you're imagining things, chicken shit."

Winnie took one.

"Then who dug that tunnel, Mr. Smartypants?"

Digging his lighter from his pocket, Tommy lit Winnie's cigarette, then his own.

"Who knows?" Tommy shrugged, then leaned back and blew smoke into the air. "Probably always been there, since the shack was built, like maybe a century ago. An escape route, or secret entrance, somethin like that."

" A *century* ago? Fast food? Fountain sodas with lids and straws? Plastic forks?" Winnie mocked. He was smiling hugely, reveling in the payback.

"Okay, asshole," Tommy retorted, smiling back. "I'm talkin a century ago that it was *built*. Hell, *anyone* could've stayed in there, or ate in there, over the last few years and left all that crap laying around everywhere—hikers, campers, a homeless guy, people partyin, whatever."

"Well, maybe. But I don't like it. And it's fine with me if we never go back." Winnie said, now blowing his own smoke.

"Like I said: chicken shit."

They paddled awhile in silence. Then Winnie spoke up:

"Think we should tell anyone?"

Tommy stopped paddling, holding the dripping oar motionless in the air, looking back at Winnie.

"Probably not. They'll either think we're lyin, or crazy, or we might even get in trouble cuz they'll wonder what in the world we were doin all the way out there. And besides, we'd have to tell 'em bout this boat, and then they'd probably take it away or think we stole it or somethin, and that would suck. So no, we should probably just keep it to ourselves."

With that, he turned and continued paddling.

Winnie smiled. "So it'll be our little secret, huh?"

Without turning, Tommy smiled too.

"Yep. One of many."

•

"So that's it," Tommy concluded. "Nothin much to tell, really, seein as we never actually *saw* anything there. But we *heard* somethin, like your dad did. And I wonder if whatever *we* heard is the same thing your dad heard, too. Somethin that lives out in Black Woods. Or maybe lives in that shack in the woods by the creek, and just hunts in Black Woods. Like they say in all the stories."

"Well I'll be damned." Joey said, finally uncrossing his arms. "You two might have just had the first sighting around Black Woods in years. You'll be famous, you lucky bastards!"

Winnie's eyes widened. "You really think so?"

Joey turned and walked toward the door of the shop.

"I'm gonna go tell my dad right now," he said without looking back. "And you can bet by mornin he'll have a huntin party together. They'll go out lookin for that shack, and for whatever you heard while you were there...and for whatever *he* heard stalkin him along the bank down in Blackwater. And word'll spread, you know how this town is, can't keep somethin like this a secret, no way. You guys'll probably get in all the papers —even that stupid tabloid everyone reads, *Hope To Tell*—they thrive on this kinda shit."

"But I thought you said your dad won't talk about it," Tommy called back.

Joey opened the door, then stopped and looked back.

"That was when it was just him. Probably just didn't wanna sound like a fool, or especially that he was scared. But now that somebody *else* heard the same thing out there, and saw some weird shit, too—well...that's different. Now he's got an excuse to go back out there lookin for it, and can take his hunting pals with him, cuz now they won't think he's crazy."

With that, he disappeared inside.

As the boys mounted their bikes, Winnie asked, his voice hopeful: "You think he's right? We'll get in all the papers? Even *Hope To Tell*?"

"Doubt it. I think he's mostly full of crap."

"Too bad...it'd be cool to get in the papers."

Ammo in hand, the boys peddled up Fifth Street, hooked a right on Homestretch, and headed...well, home.

•

By mid-afternoon, they were back up in their hunting field, fully ammoed up.

But as usual, their hunt was disappointing. Winnie had a shot at a Blue Jay sitting in a sapling, but missed, prompting the bird to dart across the field to the woods, scolding them the whole way.

They started to give chase, but couldn't catch up with it, so they stopped short of the woods, resting beneath the big oak. But just as they turned away to head back out into the field, a squirrel began chattering at them from above, perched high on a branch that dangled out from the tree line.

The boys quickly pulled and aimed, but the quick little critter scurried down the branch and disappeared to the backside of the tree before they could release. The boys ran toward it, Wrist-Wrockets stretched tight and at the ready—but slowed to a stop at the tree line.

They stood looking up at the wall of trees, taking it in.

The thick woods loomed ominously before them like a gargantuan creature lying in wait. At the tree line, the bright summer sunshine suddenly ended—as if somehow simply chopped off—and a gloomy darkness began. Inside, old gnarled tree trunks huddled closely together, ghoulish and angry, their ancient branches intertwining high above, creating a nearly solid canopy. What little sunlight managed to penetrated the shroud of secrecy only added to the overall spookiness of the woods, slanting down in razor-thin blades that swirled with mist and dust and a host of tiny, creepy-looking flying insects.

As they stood peering into the dark depths, an eerie hush seemed to fall over not only the woods before them, but the entire field behind them as well. It was almost as if the boys were being watched, and all of nature was collectively holding its breath, waiting to see what horrific thing was about to happen.

The boys turned to one another, trepidation in their eyes.

"I'm gonna go get that squirrel," Tommy finally announced, turning to enter the woods.

But Winnie grabbed his arm.

"We can't go in there," he whispered. "That's Black Woods."

"Yeah? So?"

"What about the monster?" Winnie reminded.

"Jeez, Winnie! There is no monster! Get over it!

"But we don't know! Nobody knows!"

"Look, my old man says it's all bullshit, says the old codgers around town just make that stuff up to scare everyone—especially kids. And if you think about it, Mr. Scaredy-Cat, it's probably just a clever way to keep kids like us from wandering into Black Woods, that's all."

A little embarrassed, Winnie looked down, absently pushing a rock around with his foot. Then, in a small voice:

"But what about...you know...all those sightings? All those people who say they've seen it...?

"I don't know...they probably just saw a bear or something. Except we don't really have bears around here, either, so who knows what they saw."

"Well, all those people must have seen *somethin* in there," Winnie protested. "And people say they saw it walkin *upright* too, like a man...or like Bigfoot!"

"Dude, I'm tellin ya, it's all just talk. There's no monster living in there. My dad says so. And so does Hank, Joey just said so, remember? And besides, there's no such thing as Bigfoot."

With that he continued toward the tree line.

Winnie fell in behind him.

"Still, they've never found him—or *it*—so they don't know *what* it is! And what if—*whatever it is*—is hidin in there right now, just waitin for some kids like us to go in there, and—"

Winnie stopped in his tracks, riveted with fear.

Becoming impatient, Tommy stopped and turned back.

"I told you, there's no monster! There's not even any such *thing* as monsters! Jeez, I stopped believing in monsters when I was like four—about the same time as I stopped believing in Santa Clause, the Tooth Fairy, and the Easter Bunny. You're tellin me you still believe all that crap?"

Winnie stared at Tommy, pushed his glasses up.

"No, not really I guess."

"Okay. So let's go."

Tommy turned back to the woods, but Winnie didn't move.

"Okay, so what if it's *not* a monster, like you say? What if it's a *man*? A serial killer, or a kidnapper, or a child molester or something? Some crazy guy or homeless guy, that's living in the woods, starving, looking for something to eat—like *us*?" What if it's whoever's stayin in that old shack we found down there?"

Tommy turned back around.

"Well, if there *is* a man somewhere in there—and I'd say he'd pretty much *have* to be crazy, to be livin in these woods, or even in that old shack—then we'll just shoot him if he comes anywhere near us."

He held up his Wrist-Wrocket, smiling in confidence.

Resigned, Winnie joined his friend at the tree line.

"Well, I suppose we could do that—but I doubt these little ball bearings'll do much to stop a *crazy* guy. In the movies, they shoot 'em with *guns*, and half the time it still doesn't stop 'em!"

"Dude, that's just in the movies. That's not real."

"Okay, then, what about Jimmy Walsh? He always carried that switchblade with him—and he was *sixteen*—and he still disappeared. So if it was a crazy guy in the woods that got him, then that knife must not've done much good, huh?"

"What? Jimmy Walsh? You think he was attacked, or kidnapped, by a crazy guy living in the woods? Come on."

Winnie shrugged. "I don't know. *Nobody* knows what happened to him. He just disappeared that one day. Been missing ever since."

"I think Jimmy ran away is all. He got caught smokin pot at school, under the football bleachers, remember? He probably knew he was in super-big trouble, since his ol' man's a big-wig on the school board and all. Figured he was in for a real hidin, probably get grounded for life—and for sure would be kicked off the football team, and he was supposed to *start* that season. So he split. Took off. Plain and simple."

Just then, thunder rumbled far off in the distance.

"Shit, a storm's comin," Winnie said.

They both stepped a few feet away from the trees, and peered across the field into the southern sky. Sure enough, dark storm clouds loomed on the horizon, bruised and swollen.

Winnie let out a low whistle.

"Damn, looks like serious business," Tommy observed.

"Yeah, we better head back," Winnie suggested, trying his best to sound disappointed rather than relieved.

Cupping his hands around his mouth, Tommy shouted into the woods: "Lucky squirrel! Next time, you're mine!"

As he hollered, a flock of sparrows burst from the treetops, startling the boys. They snapped their attention upward, watching as the birds scattered and disappeared further into the woods.

"Weird. I didn't even see them up there," Winnie said.

"Or *hear* them, either. *That's* what's *really* weird. Like they were just sittin up there all that time, watchin us."

"Yeah. And I wonder why we're seeing them everywhere all of a sudden? Flocks of sparrows, I mean."

"That's right—there was a flock of sparrows at the shack we found, remember? Down at the other end of the tunnel? They took off when we came out."

"Yeah—and Joey said a flock of sparrows got flushed from a tree down in Blackwater, when that thing—whatever it was— was stalking Hank, too."

"Yeah...pretty weird, huh?"

"Sparrows, sparrows, everywhere," Winnie jingled, as he peered all about into the treetops above.

With that, the boys turned and trudged back toward the bridge. And as they went, the strange silence suddenly lifted; all the normal sounds of nature—the birdsong, the cicadas, the chatter of squirrels—returned to the field.

As they approached Old Rope, they stopped about twenty yards short and simultaneously clicked the buttons on the bottoms of their Wrist-Wrockets, folded them in half, secured the rubber tubes, and slipped them into their back pockets before continuing toward the bridge in silence.

But then, they again stopped in their tracks, this time at what they heard: off in the distance, a tune—vague, nearly imperceptible—wafting to them from across the canyon.

Could it be....?

As the two stood motionless, a light melody danced across Hope Creek Canyon from the town side—at first piecemeal, as it wrapped itself around the clustered houses, the cars parked in driveways, the pickup trucks parked in the streets. Growing stronger as it neared, the many dispersed fragments melding back together, again solidifying into one, before traveling up Silver Hills, across the canyon, and to their ears.

The boys listened intently, and yes! It was indeed that magical melody that always enchanted and delighted children everywhere: the unmistakable, happy little tune of...

...the ice cream truck!

Upon confirming the sound, the boys looked at each other in googly-eyed excitement.

"It's gotta be in The Flats," Tommy guessed.

"Yep. Sounds like it's pretty close, too!"

Not another word needed to be said, for it was understood:

If they didn't hurry, they were gonna miss it!

The day's fruitless hunt already forgotten (*mission accomplished*), they ran full-bore the rest of the way to the bridge, tripping and stumbling over the rough terrain.

It was a hot, windless day, and Old Rope lay idle before them, so they hesitated only a moment before venturing on.

After trotting across the rickety bridge, they hurried down Silver Hills towards civilization with visions of *dreampops* and *fudgesicles* dancing in their heads.

•

When they burst from the brush onto the old nameless road on the edge of town, they couldn't believe their luck: the ice cream truck was *right there*, on the north end of the street, facing them, music blaring, a handful of kids gathered at its side waiting to order.

It must have just stopped, because the driver, an old man who all the adults in town simply referred to as "Wilson"—and none of the kids knew whether that was his first or last name— was still in the driver's seat. He threw a lever, triggering the big yellow CAUTION: CHILDREN CROSSING sign to swing out from the side of the van.

The boys waved at him, and he waved back through the windshield as he stood, reached up and flipped a switch to turn off the music, then turned and worked his way between the bucket seats and back to the order window.

The boys hurried up the street as the other kids crowded around the side of the van, money in hand.

The kids in front dispersed one at a time as they received their treats, leaving Tommy and Winnie alone at the window when it was their turn. After scanning the old chipped and paint-flaked menu off to the side, Tommy ordered a *Bomb Pop*, and Winnie of course ordered an ice cream sandwich, always his favorite.

After rummaging around in the chest freezer behind him, Wilson brought the treats to the window.

"These together or separate?"

The boys looked at each other, then shrugged.

"Might as well be together," Tommy said, as they dumped their pocket change together onto the tiny counter protruding from under the window.

"Okay, two-eighteen then."

Tommy counted out some coins, then slid them across as Winnie plucked his unused coins off the counter.

Tilting his head back to see through the bottom of his bifocals, the old man scrutinized the coins in his hand, nodded in satisfaction, then tossed them in the register.

"Perfect. And there ya go, boys," he said cheerily, handing the cold treats through the window.

"Thanks, Wilson!" they said in unison, each taking their treat from the counter. But when they turned to leave, the old man stopped them.

"Say, uh...I saw you boys come outta them woods up the street there."

The boys looked at each other, wondering what was up, if maybe they were in trouble.

"Yeah, so?" Tommy said.

"Well, I was just wondering if you guys been up in Silver Hills? Up by the canyon? You guy's ain't been playin around up there, have ya?"

Winnie clammed up, afraid now, but Tommy answered.

"Well, we don't play right around the canyon, no sir. We go across the bridge to the field on the other side. That's where we go to hunt."

At that, Winnie jabbed him in the ribs with his elbow.

"With our slingshots," he added.

"Old Rope?" The man gasped. "You two been goin across Old Rope? That's mighty dangerous, y'ask me. They shoulda took that damn thing down years ago!"

Winnie piped up: "It's no big deal, really. Specially on a day like today, when it's calm, no wind or anything."

As if to refute this, thunder rumbled again, closer now, and a breeze kicked up, noticeably cooler than the hot, heavy air that had stifled the day up until now.

"Well, calm or not, you boys shouldn't be playin around up there. It's too close to Black Woods. You should stay far away from them woods, far as you can get. They're evil. Dangerous. Never know what could happen."

"It's okay, Tommy shrugged. "My dad says there's nothin—"

"I lost my daughter to them woods," the man interrupted. "forty long years ago, back when she was just a little girl. It's true you know, what they say, the stories about the missin kids. I know it, first hand, cuz my little Charlotte was one of 'em that went missin. Black Woods is haunted, y'ask me. Somethin evil livin in there. Or maybe the woods themselves is evil."

Eyes wide, the boys looked at each other.

"You lost your daughter in Black Woods? She's one of the missing kids?" Winnie asked.

"Hang on a sec," the old man replied, holding up an index finger. Turning, he shuffled to the front of the van. Reaching over the driver seat, he turned the key, killing the engine with a sputter and shake, then returned to the window.

"I don't like to talk about it—fact is, I *haven't* talked about it for years, try to forget about it, but it don't matter, I can't never forget what happened—but if it'll help keep you kids from goin back up there, make you understand the stories are true, that the danger is real—then I'll tell ya what happened to me and my little girl Charlotte so many years ago, bless her soul."

The boys stood transfixed, unopened ice cream in hand.

He turned and slid a stool over from the back somewhere, sat down, crossed his arms in the window. He sat there for a moment, as if thinking it over, then let out a long sigh. Turning, he opened the freezer behind him, pulled out a *Big Dipper* ice cream cone, zipped the wrapper off in one pull, and took a bite, tiny bits of crushed peanuts sprinkling down onto the counter. Chewing, he looked up at them over his glasses, and began:

"It happened in the spring of thirty-five—like I said, forty years ago..."

•

Spring had arrived early, and a beautiful Saturday was in the making. Warm, breezy, big puffy clouds in the sky. The world was coming back to life, after hibernating through a long, harsh winter.

That morning, the Women's Literary Club was holding it's monthly Book Talk at the library, so Liz Wilson had headed out directly after breakfast, her tabbed and notated copy of Stark Young's *So Red the Rose* clamped confidently under her arm. Since Claire was picking her up—the president of the club, and an influential member of both the Town Council and the School Board—she wore her good hat.

That left Lornell (he was named after his grandfather, who immigrated to the States from Scotland in the late nineteenth century, though today most everyone just called him Wilson) to tend to their young daughter Charlotte until late afternoon sometime. So he needed to come up with some ideas of what they could do together to pass the time. She was only eight, so his options were limited.

First, he enlisted her to help in doing the breakfast dishes. Mostly, she stacked them in the drainer after he washed and rinsed them and handed them off.

When they were finished, he stood in the kitchen looking down at her, while drying his hands with a dishtowel.

She looked up at him, blinking.

"Well, what are we gonna do now, Charlie?" he asked as he draped the towel on the front of the sink.

She shrugged, walked to the dining table, slid a chair out, climbed up in it, and sat there fidgeting with her curly blonde hair, just looking at him.

"Well, we need to do *something*," he said. "You plan to just sit there playing with your hair all day?"

"No," she said.

"Well then, what would you like to do? Up to you. It's Saturday, I'm off work till Monday, and we got all day to do whatever we want, at least till your mom comes home. Any ideas?"

"We could go fishing," she muttered, then looked sheepishly down at the table.

"Fishin? You wanna go fishin?" he asked, incredulous.

"You go fishing all the time, and I never get to go with you," she mumbled, still avoiding his eyes.

"You wanna go fishin with me?" he asked, still not believing his ears. "Since when?"

She shrugged. "I dunno. Lately."

"Well I'll be...looks like you're a Wilson, after all! Fishin's probably in your blood! Definitely runs in the family!"

"So...can we go? Just this once? *Pleeeeaaaase* Daddy?"

"Huh. You're serious, aren't you?"

She shook her head quickly, blonde curls bouncing.

He shrugged. "Well, I don't see why not. Let's go fishin! And afterward, for lunch, how about we have ourselves a nice little picnic? Perfect day for it!"

Charlotte threw her arms into the air in victory. "Yaaaaay!"

"But first, I suppose we should go get you some fishin gear."

"Okay!"

Then he looked her over. She was wearing a pink dress.

"Well, first off, you can't be fishin in a pink dress, can ya? No, I don't think so. So why don't you go change—put on some-thin won't matter if it gets dirty, or wet—while I fix us some lunch to take with us?"

"Okay." She slid off the chair and hurried down the hall.

Just as he finished packing the picnic basket with peanut butter sandwiches, four bottles of Coke, and paper bag full of home-made chocolate chip cookies, she emerged from the hall re-clad in an older, faded denim knee-length dress, and the cutest little pink and white sunhat he'd ever seen.

"Where'd you get that hat?" he asked.

"Mommy got it for me last summer for when we go to the park. So I don't get sunburned."

"Huh," he said. "First I've seen it. Looks awful cute on ya."

"That's what Mom always says."

He had her carry the basket and a folded-up blanket out-side and put it in the cab of the truck (which he always called "Ol' Double-A", but she didn't know why) while he fetched his fishing hat from the top shelf in the coat closet and the rest of his gear from the storage area in the back of the laundry room.

Outside, he loaded the gear into the back of the truck. As an after thought, he went to the side of the house and grabbed a bucket from under the spigot, dumped what little water was in it out on the grass, and threw it in the back too.

"What's that for?"

"You'll see."

They got into the cab, he started her up, and they headed out to Jason's.

•

The bell above the door jingled as they pushed into *Jason's*

Jigs Bait & Tackle Shoppe, Lornell holding the door open and Charlotte slipping in under him.

"Mr. Wilson!" Jason greeted from back behind the counter. "Good to see ya! Been awhile!" Looking down at the little girl approaching the counter, he smiled.

"And who might this be?"

Lornell strolled up behind her. "Charlie, say hello to Jason. He owns the place."

The little girl blushed, but timidly complied.

"Hello."

"Well hello there, Charlie! Nice to meet you. And that's a mighty pretty hat you're wearin, Miss Wilson!"

He looked up at her dad, eyes wide. "This is Charlotte?" he asked, incredulous. "She was still in diapers suckin her thumb last time I saw her! Growin like a weed, ain't she?"

"And already too big for her britches, y'ask me."

"Oh, Daddy!"

Jason chuckled.

"So what can I do ya for?" he asked.

Lornell rested his hands on Charlotte's shoulders.

"Well, Charlie here needs a new setup...somethin her size. Maybe a little bigger, somethin she can grow into."

"Alright. Cane or reel?"

"I think reel'll work. Somethin simple, she can handle easy."

"Okay, I got just the thing I think, about her size. And what about tackle?"

"Nah, already got everything I need in my box. Could use a tub of red worms, though."

"Ahhh, goin out today, huh? Nice day for it, finally."

"Yep. The wife's out somewhere gabbin with her girlfriends in the literary club about books and such, so me and the little tyke here gonna take advantage, sneak out to the creek and haul in a few—"

—he looked down at the top of Charlie's head—

"—aren't we, sweetie?"

"Haul in a *bunch!*" she corrected.

Her dad chuckled, then looked back up at Jason.

"Definitely a Wilson," Jason observed, smiling down at the little girl, then back up at Lornell, locking eyes.

"Cocky, just like her dad."

He winked, and the two men smiled at each other.

•

After leaving Jason's, they drove through town to the north side of Hope Creek, crossing over on Caboose Lane, which ran parallel to the railroad tracks. As they crossed the skinny two-lane bridge, he pointed out the big steel trestle off to the right, telling her that's where the train goes across.

"It's *huge!*" she exclaimed.

Chuckling, he pulled off the road and parked in a grassy area under the shade of a big, white-barked Sycamore.

Before getting out, he turned and dug two Cokes out of the basket between them, and handed one to her. Then they hopped out, fetched the gear out of the back, and headed down the rocky embankment toward the creek. Other than rock and gravel, it was mostly just clumps of wild grass, some scattered tall weeds—so pretty easy going really.

Once they reached the bottom, they stopped on the bank of the creek, and he pointed downstream.

"See that wood pier sticking out into the creek down there, on the other side of the train trestle?"

"Uh-huh."

"That's where we'll be fishin from. Go ahead, you walk in front of me. And be careful, it can get pretty slick through here. Don't want ya fallin in."

"Okay."

Together, they walked carefully along the creek, passed under the trestle, and stepped up onto the pier, where they relieved themselves of their gear.

"This is pretty neat," she said, looking around at the pier.

"An old buddy of mine built it—Earl Richards, lives right up the hill there—we used to work together, at the shop. Put it in a few summers back during the drought. Creek dried halfway up, to where it was just a stream out there in the middle, so he took advantage and put this pier in before the thing filled back up when the rain came in the fall. Pretty smart, that's what I think. Says he plans to get a rowboat someday, too, but I don't know. He ain't around here much anymore, since he retired. Hear he bought a place down in Florida, spends most his time down there now. But the way I see it, ain't no sense lettin a perfectly good pier go to waste, is there? Might as well put it to good use, right?"

She shrugged. "Might as well."

"Now, let's see your rod there, I'll show ya how to set it up."

Settling to his knees before her, he slid his tackle box over, opened it up, and fishing lessons officially commenced.

•

Along about noon, they decided they were getting hungry.

"I've got the perfect place for our little picnic," he told her.

"Okay."

They packed up their gear, he hauled a full stringer of fish out of the creek—loaded with several bluegill of varying sizes, and one good-sized bass—and they headed back to the truck.

First thing he did was drop the two empty soda bottles into the bucket in the back, followed by the dripping line of fish.

"So *that's* what it's for!" she exclaimed.

"Catch on fast, don't ya?"

"Of course. I'm a Wilson," she said with a shrug.

Smiling, they loaded the rest of the gear.

Once he drove them back across the Caboose Lane bridge, he turned left at a sign that said The Lookout, with an arrow pointing in that direction, and headed east on Lookout Lane, a narrow two-laner that hooked south then snaked its way up the north end of Silver Hills, terminating in a roundabout near the top, where a clearing had been cut from the woods.

From up there at The Lookout, you could see nearly the entire town spread below.

Parking spaces lined the outer ring of the roundabout, and one of them was occupied. His eyes widened at the sight of the all-white Packard Convertible parked there, shiny and clean, with the top down.

A smattering of picnic tables sat around in the grass, and a family of three was occupying the table nearest the Packard. A nicely-dressed couple—the man in a white long-sleeve button-up, tan slacks, and a white fedora, the woman in a lovely white and yellow flowered dress and a white wide-brimmed sun hat —with a little red-headed boy in coveralls who looked to be about Charlotte's age, maybe a year or so older. They appeared to have finished eating, and were packing up to leave.

He parked behind the Packard and picked up the basket.

"Oh, I see!" Charlotte said, sitting up and looking through the windshield. "Picnic tables!"

"Oh, no, no," he said, shaking his head. "We can't have a real picnic sittin and eatin at a *table*, now can we? How would that be any different than eatin at the table at home?"

She thought about this for a moment.

"Guess it's not."

"Here, take the blanket. I know a better spot, up top."

When they got out of the truck, Lornell lifted a hand to the couple in greeting, approaching them as they loaded their picnic gear into the trunk of their car.

"How you folks?"

The man waved back.

"Just fine, thanks. How about yourself?"

"Good, thanks."

Seeing Charlotte approaching, the young boy walked right up to her and introduced himself.

"Hi, I'm Ted. What's your name?"

"Charlie."

"But Charlie's a boy's name," he said, looking perplexed.

"My real name is Charlotte. Charlie's just my nickname."

"I have a nickname, too. It's Red...cuz of my hair."

Charlie looked at his crop of thick, red hair.

"I like your hair."

"Red, leave her alone and come back here, help your mother load the rest of our things!" the man ordered.

"Yes, sir," the boy answered, and immediately returned to the rear of the car and started handing stuff up to his mom.

The two men shook hands.

"Lornell Wilson. That's my daughter, Charlie."

Charlotte waved timidly.

"Raymond Kelly. Or just Ray, really. My wife Nicole, and our son Ted."

The three nodded to each other as Nicole closed the trunk, walked around to the side and opened the passenger door, allowing Ted to climb into the back seat of the car.

"Have to say, that's the most red hair I've ever seen on a lad."

"Yeah, he gets it from his granddad. Dad was a full-blooded Irishman, came to the States when I was just a baby. He's got the same exact hair as pop. Didn't get it from me—"

—he lifted his hat for a moment, exposing his sandy blonde

hair, some pasted to his forehead with sweat—

"—mine's blonde, like my mom's—"

—then he placed it back—

"—you know, they say our genes skip a generation. I'd say they're right."

As he spoke, they were both looking down at the boy, who was sitting quietly in the back seat.

"Ted, say hello to Mr. Wilson."

"Hello, sir."

"Hello, son," Lornell greeted.

He looked back to Ray. "Mighty well behaved, too."

"We got lucky," Nicole said from the other side of the car. "He's a good boy. Nothing at all like his father."

They all chuckled at this, but then Ray concurred.

"Unfortunately, she's right. Ted's nothing like me, thank God. When I was his age, I was a total snot. A troublemaker in my adolescence, and a real hell-raiser as a young man, specially when I got boozed up. Got myself into plenty of trouble, too. Luckily, I met Nichole at a friend's wedding party, fell in love —and she managed to straighten me out."

He turned to her, and they smiled at each other. As she settled into the passenger seat, closed the door, and began tucking a few runaway strands of dark brunette hair up into her sun hat, he turned back to Lornell and twitched his head in the direction of his boy in the back.

"But Ted here, he's a good kid. Doesn't take after his old man. Laid back, behaves himself, seems to have a good head on his shoulders—"

—he leaned back toward the boy, raising his voice—

"—even if it IS buried under a bushel of red hair!"

"Oh, dad," the boy protested.

Smiling, Ray straightened back up.

"So apparently, he didn't get any of my idiot, irresponsible, bonehead genes. Luckily, when they say the genes skip a generation, that must mean the bad ones too. But God have mercy how *his* kids turn out, if he ever has any."

Again they all chuckled.

"That's a real nice car," Charlie said from below. Shading her eyes with her hand, she was looking it over from end to end. This also turned her dad's attention to the convertible gleaming before him in the sun.

"It sure is, Charlie," he said, looking it over himself, then up to Ray. "What year is it?"

"Thirty-one. Deluxe Eight Roadster. Love it."

"She's a beaut, that's for sure. I knew soon as I saw it you folks ain't from around here."

"Iowa," Ray said, opening his door to get in. "Mill Springs. Just spent a couple weeks out on the west coast, see the Pacific. On our way back home now. Stopped in town to gas up, saw the sign for The Lookout on our way back out, thought it'd be a good place to stop for lunch."

"It is."

"Yes, it is," Ray agreed. "Very nice."

"Well, it was nice meetin you folks. Have a safe trip home."

Lornell tipped his hat as he stepped away from the car, guiding Charlotte with his hand to do the same.

Ray started the car, the in-line eight-cylinder engine bursting to life then purring like a big cat. He put it in gear, did one loop around the circle, and they all waved behind them as they headed back down the hill.

"So you ready to eat?" he asked, looking down at her.

"Yeah, I'm starving!"

He twitched his head in the direction of the woods.

"Follow me then."

She fell in behind him as they traversed the clearing uphill toward the woods, basket and blanket in hand. As if on autopilot, he drifted to his left, and stopped at the tree line directly in front of an almost invisible path that cut into the woods. If you didn't know it was there, you'd never see it.

"I used to bring your mother up here for nice, quiet little picnics all the time, back in the day," he said.

"Why'd you stop?" she asked.

This took him aback. He stood for a moment, considering.

"Now that's a good question," he finally said, as if stumped. "Don't rightly know I guess. Maybe we just got too busy." Then he shrugged. "And besides, she's never been too fond of gettin her shoes dirty."

"Is that why she stays inside and reads all the time?"

He chuckled at this.

"I suppose that's one reason."

Bowing slightly, he gestured toward the path with his arm and open hand.

"Ladies first."

It was a short expedition through the patch of woods that separated the picnic area from the open fields atop the hill. After just a few minutes crunching through the underbrush, they stepped out into the clearing that ran along the west side of the canyon.

She followed him as he walked up close to the drop-off, where they could look right down into the canyon, see the creek tumbling through the rocks hundreds of feet below.

"Wow!" she exclaimed. "We're WAY up here!"

"Yep. Beautiful view, ain't it?"

"Sure is!"

Turning, she noticed the rope bridge dangling across the canyon down at the far end of the clearing. She pointed at it.

"Can we go across the bridge?"

"No, honey, that's probably not a good idea. Dangerous."

Then she spotted the gigantic oak, standing alone in the field just in front of the woods on the other side of the canyon, offering a huge, shady area beneath.

She pointed across the canyon at it.

"Let's have our picnic over there, under that big tree!"

"Honey, the only way over there is the bridge, and I don't—"

"PUH-LEEEEAASE, Daddy? Just this once? It's so pretty over there. And that big tree looks so lonely."

He considered it a moment, looking up at the sky as if he could actually see the wind, then scrutinizing the bridge, see how much it was swaying or bouncing as a result. But besides a light breeze, all was calm, the bridge motionless. Apparently what little breeze there was wasn't enough to affect the bridge.

"Well, I suppose that's as good a spot as any," he said. Then he looked down, pointed a finger at her. "But don't you *dare* tell your mom we went across that rope bridge, you hear me?"

"Okay, Daddy, I won't—I promise!"

"Hold my hand, and don't let go till we get across."

Hand-in-hand, they walked to the bridge, crossed over the canyon, and headed over to the big oak, ducking around its thick trunk to the other side, closer to the woods. There, he let go of her hand and motioned to the ground.

"Spread the blanket out right here."

Together they pulled and smoothed and worked the kinks and creases out, then sat, divvied up the lunch from the basket, and commenced picnicking. The sound of the creek far below wafted up the canyon walls with the warm, springtime breeze. By the time it reached them, it sounded like just a tiny, babbling brook, blending with the birdsong that drifted from the woods behind them.

About halfway into their sandwiches, they heard a loud *pop!* in the woods, off to their left, not far from where they sat under the tree. They both stopped chewing and stared into the trees, listening.

It was quiet for a moment; then they heard rustling sounds, bushes or tree branches, something.

Lornell put his sandwich down and hollered "Who's there?" in the direction of the woods. They both looked all around, trying to see or hear something, anything.

Nothing.

"What do you think it was?" Charlie asked.

He shrugged. "Don't know. Squirrel climbing around in the trees or something."

They continued eating, but then heard the rustling sound again, this time louder, closer, in the woods directly behind them. Whatever it was, it was obviously moving.

He put his sandwich down again, stood, took one step closer to the tree line, and cupped his mouth.

"Hello? Who's there? Anyone? We can hear you, so you might as well come on out! No sense sneaking around, you're not foolin anyone!"

Nothing.

Breeze blowing through the leaves above them.

Turning, he looked down at her, and she looked back up at him, worried.

He placed his finger to his lips, signaling her to be quiet.

Stooping, he picked up a good-sized rock, and threw it into the woods, in the direction of the sounds. It snapped and cracked through the brush, leaves floating down behind it.

"I know you're in there! Come out, before you get hurt!"

Then, a really loud *crack!*—like a branch snapping—but this time, further to the right, as if whoever it was—or *what*ever it was—was circling them.

He turned and pointed at Charlie.

"You stay right there, don't move. I'm gonna go check it out."

"Don't go!" she begged. "Daddy, I'm scared—don't leave!"

"I'm not gonna leave," he reassured. Bending, he picked up another rock. "I'm just gonna step inside those trees—"

—he pointed behind him with his empty hand—

"—so I can see in there a little better, make sure everything's okay. Then I'll come right back. So don't you move, you hear?"

"Okay. But hurry, okay?"

"I'll be right back. It's probably nothing anyway, just a squirrel or something. But I wanna check it out, make sure."

With that, he tip-toed across the grass, hesitated at the tree line for a moment, peering in, bobbing his head this way and that—then disappeared inside.

She waited on the blanket under the tree, eyes wide, Coke bottle clutched to her chest.

He had only taken two or three steps into the woods, but it was already so dark he could barely see any distance at all. The canopy of tree branches was so thick and interlaced it blocked nearly all the sunlight.

He peered in as far as he could, slowly scanning the area he thought the last sounds had come from. He saw nothing.

Heard nothing.

Then, he realized how truly strange that was; he actually *heard nothing*—no cicadas, no crickets, no birdsong, no scurrying or flying critters, *nothing*.

The silence was mesmerizing; he just stood, entranced.

Until Charlie screamed, that is.

High-pitched, blood-curdling, terrified.

He scream broke him from his trance. He turned, sprinted the few steps before bursting out of the woods, his daughter's name on his lips.

"Charlie—"

He stopped in his tracks.

The blanket, the basket, the food, all of it was there—but his daughter was gone. Her Coke bottle lay beside the blanket, a brown fizzing puddle spreading in the grass.

"CHARLIE!!" he yelled as loud as he could. Horrified, he glanced all around the area—the blanket, the field, even up in the tree—she was nowhere to be seen.

"CHARLIE!" he yelled again, as he started running along the edge of the woods, looking in at every possible opportunity. First one way, then the next, yelling his daughter's name into the woods with every few steps.

"CHAR—"

He stopped dead in his tracks. There, in front of him, right on the edge of the woods, in the tall grass.

Her pink and white sun hat.

Dropping the rock, he snatched up the hat, examined it. No dirt, no blood, just a hat. He put it to his nose, inhaled deeply, taking in her sweet aroma.

He tore into the woods directly at the point where her hat lay, and spent the next hour searching everywhere throughout the dense, dark trees and brush for his daughter—calling her name, over and over and over, as loud as he could, until he had no more voice.

But it was all for naught.

She was gone.

•

"Eventually, I went into town fast as I could drive, and got the Sheriff—it was Rudy back then, Rudy Shelton—and he and a young Deputy, kid by the name of Adam, I think—Adam, or Adams, don't rightly recall—came up and searched around, but they didn't find anything either, and soon it got too dark out anyways. So next day they organized a search party, police and townsfolk both, and they searched the entire area for two days. Even called in a dive team to search the creek below, maybe she'd fallen and drowned. But I knew better."

The old man popped the last of the cone into his mouth, brushed his hands together, then wadded up the wrapper and brushed the crumbs off the counter.

"Know how I knew they wouldn't find her?" he asked. "That she was gone for good?"

Too riveted to answer, the boys just shook their heads.

"The sparrows."

They both frowned, perplexed.

"See, after I searched the woods myself all that time, and decided to go into town and get the Sheriff, that's when I seen 'em—up in that big oak tree."

"Sparrows?" Tommy asked.

"Sparrows. Whole flock of 'em, just sittin up there lookin down at me. I stopped and was looking back up at them, when they all of a sudden burst from the tree and flew off into woods. And not a peep from 'em, either. Just all quiet-like. It was real creepy. But that's when I knew."

"Knew what?" Winnie asked, still perplexed.

"Oh—I don't suppose you boys know what's special about sparrows, do ya?"

They looked at each other, shrugged, looked back.

"Guess not."

With that, he leaned into the window, lowered his voice.

"You see, legend has it, sparrows can catch the souls of the recently departed. So I suspected that flock I seen was carrying the soul of my little girl. I *sensed* it."

The boys again looked at each other, eyes wide.

"Wow," they whispered, then turned back.

"And they *know*, too. That's what's really special about 'em. They know when it's about to happen, when someone's about to give up their soul. So they wait nearby. So if you ever see a whole flock of sparrows just sittin around, like they're waitin for somethin, that's probably just what they're doin—waitin for someone's soul, that they know is about to die."

With that, he sat back up out of the window, then turned and tossed the wadded wrapper back into the van somewhere.

As he did so, the boys once again turned to each other.

"You thinkin what I'm thinkin?" Tommy asked quietly.

"Sparrows, sparrows, everywhere," Winnie jingled softly.

Apparently not having heard them, the old man turned back and continued:

"So I knew, when I seen them sparrows, they weren't ever gonna find my Charlotte. She was gone, whatever evil lurks in them Black Woods took her from me, and I've never seen her since. Just hear her voice at night."

"You hear her voice?" Tommy asked.

"Yep, at night. No doubt about it, it's her. That same scream I heard when I was in the woods that day and she disappeared. For forty years now, I been hearin her scream, over and over, like a nightmare I can't wake up from."

The boys looked at each other, eyes wide, then back.

"So it's true what they say?" Winnie asked. "The screams of the missing kids can be heard at night, around Black Woods? It's their ghosts or something?"

"Oh, absolutely. For a long time, it was just Charlie. That's cuz she was the first—I wish she wasn't, cuz then I'da known better than to take her anywheres near them evil Black Woods. But over the years—seems to be about every eight or ten years, I reckon—another child disappears, and another voice joins the chorus. I lost track, but it's up to four or five now I think. And you can hear their ghosts—or their souls, or whatever they are —screamin at night. Hear it all through the woods, even down the hill sometimes."

Winnie let out a low whistle.

"You boys remember Nicky? Nicholas Hughes? He was the last one to go, vanished about...well, I'd say it's been going on ten years ago now."

They told him they'd heard some stories, but were way too young back then to actually remember anything.

"Well, he was about your age, and he and a friend were messin around up there by that bridge. Ends up, Nicky went across, but his friend—Douglas something or other, or maybe Douglas was his last name, I don't rightly recall, he don't live here no more anyways, went in the military right out of high school—anyway, he was scared to cross. What I hear, Nicky stood on the other side—there by Black Woods, dontcha know —taunting his friend, calling him all manner of names trying to get him to cross over. But he just ended up crying at Nicky's bullying and left, went home. But Nicky never made it back home, and nobody's seen the boy since. Disappeared, just like the rest. Just like my little Charlotte. Just up and vanished."

"Wow. I hadn't heard that." Tommy mumbled.

"Me either." Winnie added.

"So that's why I'm tellin ya, you two shouldn't be messin around up there. In fact, you shouldn't be goin anywhere *near* Black Woods. *Especially* now."

"Why not now?" Tommy asked.

"You boys don't listen very well, do ya? Typical kids. I just got done tellin ya these kids been disappearin bout every eight or ten years, didn't I? Well, last one was goin on ten years ago... that means it's about time for the next. Neither of you wants to be next, do ya?"

"No sir," they both chimed in unison.

"Well then, you stay away from them woods, you hear?"

"Yes sir," they again chimed in unison.

The man stood from his stool, and slid it off to the side.

"Now, go eat your ice cream fore it melts all over ya."

The boys had forgotten all about their ice cream, and looking now, were surprised to see the packages in their hands dripping in the grass. They both started quickly unwrapping their treats, holding them at a distance so they wouldn't drip on their clothes.

As they did so, thunder rumbled in the distance.

"And you best head home, fore ya get rained on."

"Yeah, that's where we're headed," Tommy said. "Winnie lives right over on Hillsboro."

"All right then. Guess I'll see you boys next time I'm in the neighborhood."

The old man turned away from the window to leave, but Winnie called after him.

"Hey—can I ask you a question?"

Tommy just looked at his friend, curious.

Inside the van, the man turned back. "Sure. What is it?"

"Why does everyone call you Wilson?"

The old man looked stunned. Giving Winnie a perplexed look, he replied: "Why, cuz that's my name! Why else?"

He smiled, winked, and without another word headed up to the front of the van and climbed into the driver's seat.

The boys looked at each other, shrugged, and walked away smiling as the van started up, the caution sign folded in, and the van did a grinding U-turn in the old crumbled road and headed back into the neighborhood.

Once it turned the corner, the music started back up, the

happy jingle echoing all around the small clapboard houses and fading away.

•

The boys stood on the side of the road, eating their ice cream in silence, thinking about what Wilson had told them.

Thunder rumbled in the sky, a little closer this time.

"That's weird, what he said about the sparrows," Winnie said. "After we were just talkin about seein 'em so much lately."

"Yeah...but you know what really gets me? That that Nicky kid was playin up there in the same field where we hunt when he disappeared," Tommy said.

"Yeah, and he was our age, too," Winnie added.

Walking over to the closest driveway, they dropped their wrappers into a trash can that stood awaiting collection.

Then Winnie froze, as a thought occurred to him.

"Hey—"

Tommy gave his friend an inquisitive look.

"Speaking of our age—isn't tomorrow your birthday?"

Tommy sighed dejectedly as he stooped and picked a small rock up from edge of the road. "Yeah..."

He flung the rock side-armed into the woods across the street, the boys listening as it tore through the foliage.

Then Winnie bent and selected a rock of his own.

"What's the matter? You don't act very excited."

"That's because I'm not."

Winnie stopped mid-throw, his arm raised up behind him, and looked over at Tommy.

"C'mon, it's your birthday...it's supposed to be a *good* thing."

He turned and flung the rock high and hard. They both watched the small, spinning silhouette soar into the bright sky, then descend into the tops of the trees, where it disappeared with a falling sequence of soft thuds. A perturbed blackbird burst from within, twittering loudly as it flew off to find refuge elsewhere.

"Nice one."

"Thanks."

They turned and started toward Winnie's house.

"Well normally, it *would* be a good thing...problem is, it's my *thirteenth* birthday—and at my house, everything changes when you turn thirteen."

"Oh, that's right—the farm."

"Uh-huh."

•

At Tommy's house, the standing rule was that once you turned thirteen, you were no longer considered a *child*, but a *teenager*—the first stage toward manhood—and that meant you started working the family farm. Not that Tommy and Will didn't already help out; they did, performing many chores: collecting eggs, milking cows, the typical yard work, house work, helping their dad with the machinery, etc.

But once the boys reached that dreaded age of thirteen, the farm became their full-time job.

Hard work.

In the fields.

All day.

Edgar Baker was a poor farmer (in both senses); a stingy penny-pincher, he always claimed he couldn't afford to hire farmhands—not even the seasonal migrant workers—although he somehow managed to afford a seemingly endless supply of booze and cigarettes.

So, on the Baker farm, slave labor it was.

And he had no problem cracking the whip when needed— or even when not; Edgar Baker was not only a poor farmer, but a poor father as well.

And on top of all that, he was also a poor husband; in his countless drunken fits, he'd harassed and beaten his wife to the point she'd up and left them all in the middle of the night, back when Tommy and Will were just toddlers. They'd not seen or heard from her since.

Though the boys were devastated when she left, their dad wasn't; instead, he actually seemed *glad* she was gone.

"At least now a man can get some peace and quiet around here," he said flippantly. "Couldn't cook worth a shit anyhow."

And that was it; life on the Baker farm went on.

Then, three years ago, Tommy's older brother Will suffered the misfortune of turning thirteen. And Tommy still remembered their father's words the night of Will's ill-fated birthday:

"Bill, startin tomorrow, there'll be no more free-loadin around here. Uh-huh, ya heard me right, I called ya Bill, cuz that's your name, here on out. Will is a boy's name, and you ain't a boy no more, you're a man. And come tomorrow, Bill Baker, you're to start actin like one—and workin like one."

And from that point on, their father not only stubbornly refused to call his son *Will*, but even prohibited Tommy from addressing his brother by any name other than *Bill*, so hellbent was he to demonstrate to both boys that Will was no longer a child, but a man, and must therefore work.

And work hard.

When they were alone together, Tommy still called his brother *Will*—but it wasn't long before Tommy figured out that *Will* had pretty much gone away anyway; someplace far away, someplace on the *inside*—and left behind an empty husk called *Bill*.

And this saddened Tommy tremendously.

His missed his big brother.

The farm work was grueling, and unrewarding. Sunup to

sundown, in the heat, in the rain—even in the snow, if winter came on and harvest was running late—which it usually was.

And, to make things worse, the Baker farm possessed very little modern equipment. Most of their equipment was rusty, or in disrepair, or just plain inoperable—so *Bill* was forced to make up for much of their father's lack of proper maintenance and preparation through long, hard manual labor.

Tommy had witnessed first-hand what happened to his brother, once he started working the farm.

Will changed, withdrew—and slowly became this new *Bill*. And he didn't like what he saw.

Not one bit.

But after that first season, his big brother seemed to surface for awhile, became the old *Will* again—only with a wary, nervous aspect about him that Tommy thought was strange and not like *Will* at all. He noticed his brother's eyes darting about the room while he constantly tapped his foot or jiggled his leg, like he'd developed some kind of nervous tic. He couldn't seem to sit still.

Edgy.

Skittish.

Like a long-tailed cat in a rocking chair factory.

Then, during the second season, *Will* went under for good. Never resurfaced.

So for the last two years, *Bill* was completely withdrawn, nearly catatonic. He had also started sneaking cigarettes and booze from their father, and whenever he got caught, the punishments were severe.

Will called them *whippings*;

Tommy called them *beatings*;

The old man called them *lessons*;

And *Bill* called them *worth it*.

Whatever you wanted to called them, they were nearly un-bearable to Tommy. He couldn't even imagine how *Will* was able to take them, over and over and over.

Eventually, *Bill* started acquiring his cigarettes and booze elsewhere (Tommy never knew where and didn't ask). Late at night, he lay in bed and watched in silent awe as his brother disappeared out the bedroom window, then returned in the wee hours reeking of smoke and liquor. Sometimes he came back beat up, bruised and bleeding; again, Tommy never asked —and *Will* never bothered to explain.

Surprisingly, their father never remarked about *Bill's* occa-sional black eye, split lip, or facial abrasions; maybe he thought he'd inflicted it on the boy himself, during one of their *lessons*.

To make things worse, over time their father started doing a lot more drinking and smoking himself—and thus a lot less working, now that *Bill* was taking up some (actually *most*) of the slack.

And all this had been a *lesson* for Tommy; he knew that it would one day be *his* turn, and he already dreaded hearing his father's words:

"Tom, startin tomorrow, there'll be no more free-loadin around here. Uh-huh, ya heard me right, I called ya Tom, cuz that's your name, here on out. Tommy is a boy's name, and you ain't a boy no more, you're a man. And come tomorrow, Tom Baker, you're to start actin like one—and workin like one."

And now, it was here. Tomorrow, Tommy turned thirteen.

And he didn't like what was coming.

Not one bit.

•

"Well, at least you'll get paid, right?"

"Shit. You kiddin?" He refuses to even hire the immigrant workers—even for harvest. Don't wanna pay 'em, says they're all a bunch of lazy, good-for-nothin mooches. So he's sure as hell not gonna pay *us*—we're supposed to be *earnin* our keep."

"Wow. That sucks."

"Tell me about it."

Cutting through the nearest yard, they both jumped as a rabbit suddenly exploded from under a bush near the house and darted past them and across the street, heading for the woods on the other side.

They both reached back for their Wrist-Wrockets simultaneously, like two gunfighters racing to the draw (Winnie with his left hand, Tommy with his right), when Tommy suddenly stopped in horror at what he felt: *his Wrist-Wrocket was gone!*

Winnie already had his shot loaded and was stretched to maximum extension, gently pivoting back and forth as he targeted the darting prey ahead of him—while Tommy spun around like a dog chasing his own tail, grappling at both of his rear pockets in disbelief.

Winnie let go, but his shot skipped off the asphalt behind the rabbit just before it disappeared into the woods.

Finally noticing the antics of his friend, Winnie turned to him with a quizzical look on his face.

"What are you doing?" he asked. "You didn't shoot at it."

"It's *gone!*" Tommy yelled. He was bent around awkwardly, trying to see his backside as he searched for the slingshot.

"What's gone?" Winnie asked, not understanding. Then his eyes widened. "You mean your Wrist-Wrocket? What do you mean it's gone?"

"I don't know!" Tommy yelled back, in horror. "I put it in my back pocket, same as you, before we left the field—but now it's gone!"

A panicked scouring of the ground immediately around them followed, but their search did not reveal any errant

Wrist-Wrockets.

Tommy was devastated.

"I gotta go back," he said matter-of-factly.

He turned to go, but Winnie grabbed his arm.

"You can't go back now—it's getting dark." He pointed up to the sky, which was now dark and rumbling. "And besides, the storm is almost here!"

Tommy shook his arm free, and continued walking. "That's exactly why I gotta go back *now*—so I can find it before it gets too dark, and try get back before the storm hits."

He turned and ran down the street, to the point where they cut off into the woods and headed up the hill.

Winnie ran to catch up, concern building in his voice.

"But you don't even know where you lost it! Why don't you just wait, and we'll go back and look for it tomorrow, when it's light out and there's not a big-ass storm comin?"

Tommy stopped and turned to his friend.

"Look—I'm goin back *now*, all right? Stop worrying. I'll be back before it gets dark. And before the storm hits."

As if to refute this statement, the sky flashed brilliant white, thunder roared directly above them, and the wind picked up.

As he looked into the woods, and the hill he was about to climb, Tommy suddenly realized that their paths were about to split—Winnie cutting west across the open yards to his house on Hillsboro Lane, and Tommy cutting east through the thin swath of woods, then up Silver Hills and across the rope bridge to the field, where he thought he must have dropped his Wrist-Wrocket, probably when they were running toward the bridge in all their excitement over the ice cream truck.

"You better get going, then. And *hurry*," Winnie warned.

"No sweat. I'll go find it, that way I'll have it for next time."

But Tommy knew, deep down inside, there wouldn't be a

next time. Not after today, not after he turned thirteen. Starting tomorrow, everything was going to change—even his very name, from Tommy to Tom—and he was already preparing himself for it, bracing for it, both mentally and emotionally.

As he stood looking into the eyes of his best friend, Tommy suddenly felt strangely distant. As thunder rumbled overhead, filling the silence, he felt a change coming over him.

A hardening of the heart.

"So I guess this is it," he finally said, shrugging. "Don't know when I'll be able to go out huntin with you again, Commander Winston."

"But we'll still have Saturdays, right? The weekend?" Winnie asked, hope filling his voice.

But Tommy shook his head. "Farmin's seven days a week."

There was another silence, and Tommy felt himself growing even more distant, more indifferent. In a way, he was glad —it all seemed much easier that way.

"So...seeya when school starts?"

"Yup. When school starts."

But Tommy knew that this, too, was a lie.

He and Winnie had been best friends for years; Winnie was a few months younger than him, and that never made any difference before. But now, even though nothing much really *seemed* to be changing—in reality, *everything* was changing.

Tommy knew that their friendship—at least the fun, youthful, unguarded intimacy they had shared until now—was over.

Tomorrow, Tommy had to start being a man.

And working like one.

And Winnie didn't.

Winnie was lucky; he lived in town, in a normal house. His parents worked normal jobs, lived normal lives. Winnie would get to remain in the utopia of childhood for a few more years; a few more summers of romping in the fields, boating on the creek, chasing rabbits; a few more summers of playing pick-up basketball games in one of his friend's driveways, or pickup baseball games down in the ball field; a few more summers of cookouts with their neighbors or family friends, of playing with his friends. Because Winnie could still *have* friends...he could even make *new* friends...maybe even a new a *best* friend.

Tommy suddenly wished he could stay twelve, could remain a boy, even if for just one more year; but he quickly dismissed the fleeting thought as reality moved in and took hold of his mind. Tomorrow he was to become a *man*, and everything he knew as a *boy* would come to an end, like it or not.

Might as well learn to like it.

Resolving himself to this, he held out his fist.

"Seeya then."

When Winnie bumped his fist, Tommy felt his love for his best friend vacate him, as if rushing down his arm and into Winnie's, for him to take home and keep forever, like a photo.

Or a memory.

Without further words, Winnie turned, stuffed his hands in his pockets, and silently walked away across the yard, his Wrist-Wrocket riding along in his back pocket. Tommy just stood and watched him go, distancing himself from his former friend; no longer knowing him, no longer loving him, no longer allowing himself to be twelve and have a best friend.

And now, suddenly, he hated him; hated him with a passion, and never wanted to see him again. He didn't really know why, or where this sudden rage came from, but that was fine; he sensed it was better this way.

Easier.

Must just be part of becoming a man, he decided.

Nodding in acceptance of this, he turned from Winnie and

started into the woods. As he did so, the sky lit up in a series of flashes, and thunder boomed above him.

Suddenly, he felt scared; not so much scared of going back up to the field with it getting darker by the minute and a furious storm bearing down—but of the life he faced upon returning home later that evening. Scared of leaving his bright, sunny childhood behind and forging onward into the dark, lonely mysteries of manhood.

Scared of turning out like his brother.

Or worse—his father.

As if on cue, lightning flashed again, burning everything a brilliant white, and thunder roared all around him—and Tommy broke into a run.

He raced through the woods, tree branches whipping his face and neck, underbrush scraping past his knees and shins, the trees swaying in the wind behind him as if urging him on, faster and faster.

Through the woods, up the hill, into the clearing and across the rope bridge, which was starting to sway in the rising wind.

Didn't take long, either. There it was, the shiny silver frame gleaming at him from the green grass and weeds not ten feet from the other end of the bridge. He was right, it had fallen out of his back pocket when they were running toward the bridge to catch the ice cream truck.

Smiling, he picked it up, brushed it off, and returned it to his back pocket, pushing it down hard to make sure it was secure this time. But then, as he turned back to the bridge, he stopped in his tracks as lightning once again lit the darkening sky, and thunder rolled across the canyon to him as he looked at the rope bridge.

And he didn't like what he saw.

Not one bit.

He watched as the bridge shuddered, creaked, and groaned in the rising wind, mocking him as he stood there, petrified.

And he knew that the longer he waited, the worse it was going to get.

As if on cue, in that single moment of hesitation the gusts picked up even more, the storm about to unleash its full fury.

Now Old Rope danced in the wind before him, bidding him—no, *daring* him—to come cross. To Tommy, the perpetual creaking and cracking of all the brittle, decaying ropes that snaked throughout the ancient rickety boards sounded as if they were about to *snap!*, thereby plunging any hapless occupants screaming to their deaths in the rocky canyon below.

Running out of time, he knew he had a decision to make.

He needed to cross, and *quickly*. If he waited much longer, it would be too dark to see, or it would begin raining, or the bridge itself could collapse—maybe even with him on it.

But then, he again heard his father's voice:

"Come tomorrow, Tommy Baker, you're to start actin like a man—and workin like one."

The words echoed in his head—and suddenly, he wasn't so sure he wanted to cross Old Rope after all.

Why? What's the point? he thought.

Instead, maybe he could stay in paradise forever. That's it! Just stay here, in this field, hunting, exploring, playing! Winnie could even come up and visit him once in awhile. If he stayed here, maybe he could stay twelve forever, never have to grow up, never have to work the farm.

Dad and Will could work themselves to death on the farm, if they wanted to. But not Tommy.

No sir.

As he considered all this, he suddenly heard a *pop!* from a distance behind him, and turned to look back at the woods on the back side of the field.

Black Woods.

What was that? The wind? An animal? The....monster?

Now he really *was* scared...

Get a grip, he scolded himself. *There is no monster!*

He turned back to Old Rope, watching as the ancient, flimsy bridge danced and thrashed in the growing wind—and that scared him too.

But neither the monster in the woods nor the flailing bridge scared him as much as the life he faced on the farm, starting tomorrow. Or of leaving his childhood and venturing into manhood, so scared and unprepared and alone.

Is that what he really wanted? To give up everything he loved and resort to a miserable life of hard work? To risk becoming a zombie like his brother, or a drunken failure like his dad? To ultimately end up with no friends, no wife, no future?

More rustling sounds from behind. He looked again, just in time to see branches snapping back into place within the dense foliage, as if someone—or some *thing*—had moved them aside as it passed by.

And that's when he noticed them.

Above the oscillating branches, up in that giant oak tree that stood alone in the field, the faithful sentinel forever guarding the entrance to the mysterious Black Woods: sparrows.

Hundreds of them.

A huge flock, scattered among the branches, motionless.

It was the oddest thing, too: they weren't skittering about, or ruffling their feathers in the wind, or flying in and out of the tree; instead, they were all just perched solidly on the swaying branches, unmoving and silent.

Like they were watching him.

Waiting...

Really scared now, Tommy turned his attention back to the flailing bridge.

Back to his future.

And he knew it was now or never...

Then, suddenly, he understood: when you grow up, come of age, become an adult, there is a transition, a crossing over; but the child that you were before the crossing stays behind in childhood, and the adult that you become after the crossing moves on into adulthood. And once you make that transition, once you cross over, there is another element—a tiny piece of you—that is cast off, and dies. And from that point on, neither the child nor the adult are ever completely whole again. When you cross over, you lose a piece of yourself, leave it behind.

And so now he wondered: is the crossing inevitable?

Or is it a *choice?*

Perhaps there's some way around it, some way he could refuse to participate, to say no to growing up, and yes to staying twelve forever; or, perhaps there was a third option—one that would neither force him to cross into adulthood, nor force him to stay forever a child.

And then, suddenly, he realized there *was* another option—and he made his choice.

Just as it began to rain, he lowered his head and charged toward Old Rope, which now undulating wildly in the grip of the impending storm.

But he was no longer alone.

Something was behind him now, closer, he could hear it.

But he was determined not to turn around and look, or to slow down for any reason whatsoever.

Head down, he ran.

Ran to beat the devil.

But whatever was behind him was gaining on him, and

quickly—for now he not only heard it, but *sensed* it, its closing heaviness picked up by the rising hairs on the back of his neck.

Would it catch him before he made it?

He hoped not.

As he ran, the rain intensified, now coming down angry and with a vengeance, and the wind picked up to near-gale force, lightning and thunder constantly ripping at the sky.

Determined, lashed by wind and rain, he stayed the course, his head down, a low growl slowly rising from his throat and quickly escalating into a rebel yell as he ran with all his might, the unknown before him drawing ever nearer, the unknown behind him right on his heels.

Tommy's valiant cry echoed forever throughout the canyon's rocky cliffs, inflicting the small town of Hope with yet another sorrowed mystery, haunting Black Woods with yet another mournful voice, a young boy's rebellious yell forever awash in the cleansing rain that fell that evening deep into the heart of Hope Creek Canyon.